GRIND HOUSE PRESS

WARNING

The following novella includes blood, violence, gore, kidnapping, animal experimentation and death (including a mentioned child death).

An Affinity for Formaldehyde

CHLOE SPENCER

GRINDHOUSE PRESS

Grindhouse Press
PO BOX 540
Yellow Springs, Ohio 45387

Grindhouse Press #098
ISBN-13: 978-1-957504-12-4

To the ones who left their old lives behind and never looked back.

ONE

LOU REACHED TWO FINGERS INTO the back of her boot, trying to scrape out the prickly pebbles that had been bothering her the entire two and a half hour drive up from the Twin Cities. Finally free of the small rocks' tyranny, she shuddered a sigh of relief and stretched her stiff body, chipped black fingernails reaching high toward the overcast sky. She had hoped today would be sunnier. Her friend Max told her the weather was supposed to be good this weekend.

Maybe he'd meant tomorrow.

She double checked the address on her phone. Yep, this is where he asked to meet. She was grateful he'd picked out a restaurant. The only thing she'd had for breakfast was a couple of those dry-ass Belvita breakfast biscuits. The four cups of coffee she had that morning were burning a hole in her stomach and making her more nauseous than energetic. Even after stretching her limbs, they still ached for the comfort of her bed. Resting in the parking lot across from her was a restaurant, its rust-streaked sign reading, "Donna's." She could've sworn this had once been an IHOP. The blue awnings and roof, weathered from age, confirmed her suspicions. When her parents were together, they'd take her out for pancakes after church. That was back when they still cared to pretend they believed in God.

Lou gave one last good twist of her back, her spinal column crackling into place, then proceeded into the diner, the little bell dinging as she swung the door open. She flipped her aviators up on top of her head, peering around at the near-empty booths. Chipped blue-checkered tile stretched out across the floor, its surface riddled with stains and silver scratches glimmering in the light streaming in from the chunky wooden blinds. Elderly people pushed around greasy eggs and cracked their teeth on dry rye toast. She cringed when she saw one woman tenderly press her fingers against her wilted-prune lips.

Why in the hell would Max want to eat here?

"Seat yourself," a waitress said to her, a wet dish towel and cleaning bucket in hand. The towel reeked of bleach and when she slapped it onto the table, smearing the suspicious brown stains around in a queasy circle, Lou's reluctance to eat here only sunk in further.

But a promise was a promise and the Wendy's across the street wasn't open yet, so Donna's it was.

Lou sat down in an empty booth, legs spread wide, elbows resting on the table. It was the one booth in the whole place that didn't have a torn seat, nor was sticky with syrup. She looked at some of the other aged patrons, deadly silent, trying to saw through stacks of perfectly brown pancakes with water-stained cutlery. She looked in the direction of the waitress, still scrubbing at the table, who only glared back with contempt.

She sent a quick text to Max, then tried to play with the sugar and salt packets in the condiment stand, only to discover that they too were sticky. If he didn't get here soon, she was going to get sensory overload. Even the lights seemed too bright and fuzzy, like an overexposed photograph. She put her sunglasses back on and with a huff, leaned back in her seat.

The waitress waddled over to her, her back sinking under the weight of the cleaning bucket. Water sloshed from side to side and the washcloth dripped onto the floor. She swiped at her forehead with the back of her hand, brushing a few curly strands of brown hair out of place.

"A minute," she told Lou gruffly. If she was the only one working all these tables, Lou could understand her frustration.

"Could we get some waters?"

Lou stared past the waitress and locked eyes with Max, who hovered in the background, hands deep in the pockets of his mud-speckled Carhartts. She hadn't heard the bell at the front door when he walked in. He offered her a big grin, two bottom teeth shining silver. His arms stretched out for a hug. She reluctantly stood to meet his embrace and was enveloped in a plume of tires, grease, and Frito dust.

"Loulou!" he laughed, rocking her back and forth in his arms. "Wow, it's been so long. Last time I saw you your hair was red."

Lou self-consciously ran her fingers through the bleached roots of her scalp. She had gone too far the last time she tried to dye her hair and, unfortunately, burnt most of it to a chemical crisp. She last saw him five years ago, after Max visited the Twin Cities for a Kenny Chesney tour when she was attending the U of M. He had all his real teeth back then, and his hair didn't look so greasy. Greasy, or sticky? Was it sticky like everything else in this damn place?

"You had a chance to look at the menu yet? They make a mean grilled cheese. Or are you still on that vegan thing?"

"Not vegan. Pescetarian. But I'll eat a club sandwich if that's all they got."

"Hell, you wanted fish, we could've gone to McDonald's for that fish and cheese sandwich."

She scrunched up her nose at the thought of the stale fish patties. "I'd rather not."

"Yeah, you'd be fartin' up a storm all night if you had that. Reminds me of that time we went to White Castle back in junior high, remember?" He chuckled as he recalled the memory. "You ate like three of them and stank up the whole sidewalk on the walk home."

Lou blushed, glancing over at the other patrons who had obviously heard them. They shook their heads and rolled their eyes, disgusted. She remembered that day exactly: she and Max stumbled along the sidewalk, stopping every few feet so she could grab onto her knees and squeeze out some of the gas threatening to burst her stomach open. They had both laughed and cried, thinking she was about to shit her pants in the most public place possible. It was a miracle she hadn't.

The waitress finally brought their waters to them, straws inside the cups. The tips of the paper wrappers were still on top of each, wilted and wrinkly like smashed mayflies. Lou pinched the wrapper and placed it on the table. It plastered to the surface like a graffiti sticker.

"I don't plan on staying for long, so I'm not really interested in catching up."

A hurt expression crossed his face, irises stretching wide across the whites of his eyes. "Why not?"

"Because."

Lou reached into the pocket of her joggers and whipped out the crumpled purple and white invitation. Across its surface were whimsical curled letters which read:

You are cordially invited to the wedding ceremony of Mr. Max Whitfyeld and Ms. Paula Kauffman. They will be wed at the Crow Wing County Courthouse by a Justice of the Peace on July 17th, 2023 at 3PM.

"What the hell is this?" she asked.

Max blinked, staring at her as if she was the crazy one. "It's one of the wedding invitations that Paula sent out. One of the few."

"That doesn't answer my question."

"Then rephrase your question, because I'm not sure I understand you."

"Why are you marrying her?"

"Well, shit, Lou." Max twisted his baseball cap backward. He looked like he was trying too hard to be grown. "I don't know what you mean. If you love a woman, you want to marry her. I thought the gays respected that."

The use of the word "gay" in front of all the elderly people made her cringe. She rubbed her temples, aggravated. "Why are you marrying a woman that's fifty years older than you?"

He scratched the stubble on his chin. "Kinda old-people-ist of you to say."

"The word you're looking for is ageist. And—you know what, fine, I'll amend my question. Again, *why*, out of all the women in the world, are you marrying *my* grandmother?"

Max blushed and, for several moments, didn't say anything. Lou's mind festered in anger as she thought back to when they were children. In the sixth grade, she came out to Max as a lesbian, which opened an exciting dialogue between them about women. At one point, he admitted he was obsessed with Jane Fonda. At the time it had been a weird statement for him to make, but she hadn't questioned it further. She thought he meant *young* Jane Fonda; that he was attracted to staunch activists who adorned themselves in vintage clothing and had perfectly styled hair. Not old biddies approaching their early 70s.

Besides, Paula looked nothing like Jane Fonda, and the woman barely knew how to use a hairbrush. She was as wild as the forested hills she roamed. No, that romanticized her. Paula may have spent a lot of time hiking trails and walking around in the forests that surrounded this town, but she wasn't some ancient nymph bathing in rivers and basking in the warmth of nature. No. It was better to describe her as a wild dog. Tolerable if you didn't approach her, aggressive if you got too close. She was the last person anyone should ever want to marry.

"I got to know her better and . . . I don't know," Max said. "It makes sense."

"What about this makes sense? Enlighten me."

His brow furrowed in deep concentration. "Like, I don't know. We get along and she makes my life better, I guess?"

"You guess?"

"We take care of each other. Since we started dating, she convinced me to cut back on all that pop I used to drink. Probably saved me the rest of my teeth." He scratched his head. "I'm no writer. I've never been good with words. I don't know what you want me to say."

"Is there money involved?"

He snorted. "What money?"

"She sold her practice."

"Only because your dad made her do it. And it was at a loss."

"Then I'm not understanding why this is happening." Lou folded her arms against her chest. "You kiss her?"

"Every day."

"Sleep with her?"

Max blushed. "Well . . . yes."

Images of her grandmother's wrinkly naked body and Max thrusting on top of her invaded Lou's mind with a violence that left her breathless. She had to remind herself to breathe.

"What? *Why?*"

"Because, as we've already established, I love her."

Lou's voice dropped to a hushed whisper, her eyes scanning the other diners. "There're more wrinkles on the wrinkliest places of her body, if you catch my drift. Not to mention it has to be as dry and arid as a desert."

"Nothing that a bottle of *lube*," Max mouthed the word, "can't fix." He shook his head. "What're you getting at, anyways, with the wrinkles on wrinkles comment? You're going to have wrinkles someday too. We both will. Does that make us any less deserving of finding love?"

"We can *find* love, as long as it's age appropriate."

"I'm not a child, Louella."

"She knew you when you were one." Lou threw up her hands. "This feels like a manic episode or something. I mean, it can't be real."

"It's real. You know, now that she's retired, she spends a lot of her days walking around the highways and backroads looking for animals in need. Well, one night, I was driving home from the cannery and I saw her limping around by the side of the road with this little German shepherd puppy in her arms. He'd gotten dumped by some jackass in a Volvo.

"Pouring down rain. Hair plastered to her face like a second skin. Kinda reminded me of a mermaid popping up out of the water, like Ariel or something. Cold enough outside that sleet was starting to form. But there was this . . . look of determination on her face that . . . I don't know what to say. Cupid's arrow struck me dead in the heart. I pulled over to the side, helped her out, and well . . . the rest is history, really."

Lou sighed. "And when was this?"

"About a year ago."

"Only a year ago, and yet you're convinced this is what you want to do with your life?"

"I'm not getting any younger and neither is she."

"But it's my *grandmother*, Max. My *grandmother*."

"So?"

"So—Jesus, we grew up together."

"And?" He waved his hand in a circle. "We're grown up now."

"No. We're *friends*."

He shook his head. "We *used* to be friends. Then you moved away and forgot about everyone, including your own flesh and blood."

"Do you think I was obligated to stay in touch with everyone?" She ferociously scratched at her head in frustration. Her nails reopened a few scabs she had nicked into her scalp when she last shaved it. "God, Max. If you had a Facebook or even a Snapchat you'd have made it easier for me."

"I don't want any social media website stealing my information and peddling it out to every Tom, Dick, and Harry. Look up what

Zuckerberg does with your shit and tell me if you still think it's a good idea to play your little Farmville games."

"If you don't think of me as your friend anymore, why did you invite me here?"

"Because you're Paula's family," he said. "And Paula doesn't talk to your mother, and she doesn't talk to her son either. You were the only one she wanted to invite."

"So my dad knows nothing about this?"

"He'll know when we've sent out the announcements after the honeymoon." Max drummed his fingers against the tabletop. "We're going to rent a room in a little bed and breakfast in Duluth."

"How charming," she responded through clenched teeth. Her head swiveled around in search of the ornery waitress, but she was nowhere to be found.

"Besides," Max said, "we need a witness for the wedding."

"And you couldn't ask your own family?"

"In case you don't remember, Kelsea's dead."

Lou flinched at the mention of her name. Max's little sister Kelsea drowned when they were twelve. Heat flooded her face. "I-I know that, smartass. I'm talking about your folks."

"They moved to Florida, Lou. You'd know that if you called every once in a while."

"The phone works both ways."

He blinked, taken aback. Then his mouth set in a firm line. "I suppose it does. You're right."

"This is asinine. Where is she even at? Why are you the only one here?"

"She's getting ready. Had a few errands to run." He raised his hand and flagged down their waitress, who tromped over with a displeased expression, nose scrunched up like she had smelled something foul. Given how old this place looked, it wasn't hard to imagine there were unclean spaces that packed an olfactory punch. "I'll take the bacon cheeseburger deluxe, no salt on the fries, please. And she'll have . . ."

Burning in their intense gaze, Lou felt awkward, an experiment on display. She glanced down at the menu before giving an indignant huff of defeat. "A grilled cheese."

Max smiled, triumphant. "What she said."

TWO

ONE LUKEWARM GRILLED CHEESE LATER, Lou had taken about as much as she could stand of the claustrophobic diner and its mildewy, greasy stench. She didn't wait for Max to finish his cheeseburger before retreating to the parking lot, where she pretended to inspect her tires amidst vaping and internally cursing the fact she had stepped foot in this shithole town again only to serve as witness to a disgusting couple's wedding. But truth be told, while she was angry at Max, she was more upset with Paula. Typical of her grandmother to reject societal conventions—*good* societal conventions—to pursue what she wanted.

When her family all lived under one roof, there was no telling what each day would bring. Sometimes Paula would take to throwing out their Walmart-bought clothes and replacing them with thrifted things in an effort to be anticapitalist. Other times Lou would come home from school to find her conversing with stoned white people with locks, masquerading as spiritual guides and drinking "ayahuasca," which (unbeknownst to Paula) was actually watered-down purple drank. There was also the one Thanksgiving where the Butterball turkey had been replaced with twenty pounds of poorly prepared soft tofu that melted into her mashed potatoes and made everything taste like wet socks. That had been the last straw for her mother. Her father spent the next few months traveling down to the Twin Cities in search of a job until they could all flee. But the damage to their marriage—and to her family as a whole—had been dealt. They divorced days before her freshman year of high school.

Paula was not only selfish, she was a menace. She knew better than to hook up with a boy she had known since he was in diapers. Hell, it might've been since he was in utero. The very thought made her want to hack up the three slices of plastic-tasting cheese that were on that stupid sandwich.

Work boots scraped on the asphalt behind her. She didn't turn to face him. "You done?"

"I got fries if you want 'em."

"You can't bribe me with fries."

"I used to," Max said with a soft smile. "You remember that? Frybribes. Fribes."

A fribe would buy one favor or secret. If Lou wanted an extra thirty minutes to play *Animal Crossing* on Max's GameCube? Fribe. If Max wanted an answer to a question on their math worksheet that night? Fribe. Fribes were a little friendship ritual they had shared with Kelsea, too.

Kelsea. Sweet little Kelsea. What would she think of all this nonsense? In the back of her mind, Lou could almost see her face, her button nose scrunched up in displeasure for several moments before dispersing into giggles. If she concentrated hard enough she could conjure up the sound of that sweet little singsong voice. *No*, Lou told herself. *Think older*. How would *older* Kelsea feel about the fact her brother was marrying a woman that had once terrorized her?

Lou had never told Max the story—and now she didn't know why—but once when they were young and he had been busy with his paperboy route, Kelsea and Lou had decided to play catch in the front yard until he got back. Lou threw the ball too hard, Kelsea jumped for it and missed, and the ball cracked into a window, shattering it. Her grandmother came out to see what the commotion was, and even after learning it was an accident, her rage didn't subside.

Paula had smiled sweetly and picked up the baseball, still glittering with remnants of broken glass. "Kelsea, sweetie. Let me give you a refresher on how to catch a ball."

Then she whipped it at Kelsea's face, and the little girl had tumbled backward, head over heels. Lou could still hear the sound of it cracking against Kelsea's cheek, remembered the violets blossoming beneath her ivory skin and the tears streaming down her cheeks. She had run home sobbing, but nothing came from it. Lou didn't know if Kelsea had lied and said she'd been accidentally hit or if she was too afraid to tell a grownup what had really happened. Hell, with her parents—a couple of high school burnouts who lived to get drunk on weekends—they probably didn't care.

But if Kelsea had told Max the truth, he would've cared. At least he should have.

Max walked up to Lou's car and leaned against the side of it. He cracked open the styrofoam box and crunched into a fry now growing stale. For a few moments they listened to the sound of trucks rolling through the intersections and the overwhelming noises of chittering birds. A patchwork quilt of prairie fields surrounded this town and there was no escape from them.

"I know this is probably not a great way for us to wind up in each other's lives again. But I love Paula, and I want to build a life with her."

"Even though she might not have much of a life left?"

"You'd be surprised," Max said. "Paula said she feels more alive now than she ever did when she was young."

"Uh-huh."

"It would mean the world to me if we had your blessing, Lou. And your help. We can't get married without witnesses. And we could ask random strangers, but it's much more special to have people you care about there. I mean, we made a blood pact for Chrissakes. Even if we're not as close as we used to be, I still care about you."

Lou sighed. Here she had driven all this way only to realize she had no leverage. There was no way she could convince Max *not* to marry Paula, power of friendship be damned. And what was she going to do? Drive all the way back to the Twin Cities? She could do that, but damn, what a waste of a trip.

"Paula cares about you, too. You're her *only* granddaughter," Max said. "Family is family and I think you have an obligation to be here."

"An obligation?"

"This is your first time being back in over a decade. You don't approve of the wedding? Fine. But you owe it to Paula to stick around."

Lou sighed. "Fine."

"Fine?" He seemed surprised his guilt tripping worked. "Okay. Good."

She opened her car door. "So I'll follow you over to Flagstaff Road?"

"Flagstaff?" He frowned. "Oh, no. We moved a long time ago."

"She sold the house?" Damn, if there was one thing Lou had been looking forward to, it was seeing her childhood home again. Paula kept an attic full of vintage shit and there could've been something to pawn in there for a quick buck. "When did she do that?"

"A few years back, after she sold the practice." He placed his hands on his hips and shook his head, firmly disappointed in her. The way he was trying to assert himself as an authority figure skeeved her out. "See, you had to come back anyway. Too much to catch up on over the phone."

"If you say so." She sighed once more. "Lead the way, I guess."

Max hopped into his humble little pickup, parked only a few spaces away. As it sputtered to life it coughed out a cloud of black exhaust. Lou rolled her eyes, climbed into her car, and proceeded after him. The dread swelling within her body made the whole drive feel like a funeral march.

THREE

THEY TRAVELED SLOWLY DOWN THE city roads. Pickups full of hay breezed past them, along with dinky sedans full of raucous teens, windows slightly cracked, music Lou hated blasting from the speakers. Shiny storefronts, their newness distinguished by their massive glass windows, sparkled beside aged brick-and-mortar buildings with hand-painted signs. Stretches of smooth pavement gave way to cracked asphalt spotted with holes like sprinkles on a Pop-tart. The town had both grown up and regressed.

As they drove further from the town center, the yellow-and-cream-colored grasses of the prairielands grew taller and taller, guiding them through the hills and over aged dirt trails Lou remembered biking over in the summers. Max would always pop wheelies going over the bumps in the road. Half the time he was successful, and the other half he'd be adding scars to his arms and legs like his body was a sticker collection. Soon, cornfields sprouted into view. They passed the pond where she and Kelsea had once been bitten by a flock of angry geese. Years of hot summers had diminished the edges of what was once an expansive swimming hole into almost a puddle, yet the birds still floated in it, making their nests amongst the dry reeds.

She dialed up the fan on her air conditioner a little more.

Max's truck peeled around a sharp curve and she leaned into it, her wheels clipping the shoulder, kicking up a cloud of dirt in her wake. Jesus, he was going fast. Nothing out here but deer, geese, and corn, but still. She was grateful when they pulled up in front of the ranch style home, sitting in the center of the only plowed plot of land her eyes could see.

It was a confusing little place. Grecian columns separated the big red deck from the iron awning above. Moss and wisps of ivy climbed up a makeshift trellis beside the front door. Several windows were circular. Most peculiar was the collection of cacti resting in the mulched flowerbeds. Max pointed them out to her as they walked up to the front door, her suitcase in his hand.

"Aren't they pretty? All those little red flowers."

The meager flowers, more reminiscent of dryer lint than something beautiful, did not impress her. "Should cacti be in mulch?"

"I didn't want to bury them out in the yard with no rhyme or reason. Wouldn't be proper. Paula wants to hire a landscaper in the future."

He reached into his pocket and fumbled for his keys. Lou inspected the rusted white lawn furniture that occupied the space. She recognized it from Paula's old house. One time she broke a glass and Paula made her sit on one of those chairs for two hours as punishment. Bad for her ADHD, and bad for her sore little behind. Those chairs had always been uncomfortable.

Keys in hand, Max turned to face her, his lips pressed together in a thin, barely visible line. Brow furrowed in a tight knot of wrinkles and untrimmed hairs. She opened her mouth to question him, but he motioned for her to be quiet.

"Now," he mumbled, "Paula keeps . . . interesting hobbies. She means no harm by it."

"What, is it a fetish? A kink?" Did she have scantily clad photos of men plastered to the walls? That felt very Paula. She regularly rented Chippendale's videos back then. Lou remembered seeing some of the rented VHS tapes on her nightstand whenever she delivered folded laundry to her room.

"It's better if you see it for yourself."

The door's hinges screeched in protest as he shouldered it open, hoisting the luggage over the threshold and hauling it into the shadowy inside. Immediately Lou was hit with a cloud of something foul—toxic and nauseating, like sulfuric acid paired with the musk of wet fur. She twisted her head into the collar of her shirt and tried to suppress her gagging as she stepped inside.

Thin lines of light seeped in through the tangled blinds in the living room. An immediate chill overcame her, and the sound of a roaring AC unit filled her ears. Lou squinted, trying to take deep breaths waiting for her eyes to adjust. Max hovered nearby, not saying anything, his shoulders unusually stiff. In the darkness, she could see the heavy shape of something lying on the floor, ears pricked up. A dog? Paula had gotten a dog? But as Max closed the door behind her, disgust flooded Lou's body.

It *was* a dog.

But it wasn't alive.

A German shepherd, oddly enough, but full grown, curled up in a little sideways ball on the floor, its head resting between its front legs, glassy brown eyes curiously looking upward at those standing in the entryway. It was as though it had died waiting for its owner to come home, and the sad thought almost made Lou's eyes water.

"Why we gotta keep the blinds closed all the time," Max explained, closing the front door behind her. "And why it's so cold in here. If you need a sweatshirt, you let us know."

"And," Lou said, taking a shaky breath, "*how* is it better if I see all of this for myself?"

Her eyes spotted yet another animal under a console table. A beaver, standing on its hind legs, its left ear partially torn, its mouth drawn back in an odd snarl, revealing all its severely square teeth. Beside either end of the boxy Toshiba TV, two turtles gazed at one another like separated star-crossed lovers. A collection of cats, each in varying ages and colors, rested on the shelves of a disorganized bookcase.

"What the fuck is going on?"

Max pointed at her scoldingly. "I told you not to freak out."

"Why does she have so many taxidermied animals?"

"Because she's a sciencey woman, Lou. She's very interested in how the body works."

"She was a veterinarian, not an undertaker."

"Yeah, well she took up taxidermy when she wanted to make a little extra cash. Gives her something to do with her hands, too. In the fall she makes a quick buck off the bucks." He chuckled. "See what I did there?"

"How does a *buck* escalate into getting a kitten?"

Lou gestured to the soft gray one on the bookshelf, its little eyes too big for its head. Some sort of birth defect, she was sure, probably incompatible with life. Yet to see its fragile body on sacrilegious display made her stomach churn. Too many questions rose in her mind. When had this baby died, how had it died, and did Paula have something to do with it?

"Well, shit, Lou. The way she explained it, these animals would all end up in a landfill anyways. She keeps them so she can take care of them. Preserve 'em, study 'em. It's not the weirdest thing in the world, y'know. A lot of people are starting to taxidermy their pets and everything. And hell—didn't the Pharaohs do that? They wanted to be buried with their cats, right?"

"I'm surprised you even know that and . . . that's . . ."

"I'm not saying I'd want *my* cat to be taxidermied and preserved," Max said. "But she makes a good living doing it. Beats me having to pick up extra shifts."

"This is abhorrent."

"She's not fearful of death like the rest of us are. She spent an entire lifetime embracing the living and now . . ." Max shrugged his shoulders. "Now she does this. Cares for things in death. Kinda poetic if you think about it."

"If you're Edgar Allen fucking Poe," Lou spat. "Or Sylvia Plath."

"My oh my. I never took you for someone that was so judgmental."

She would've responded with, *I'd never take you as someone who refused to question the status quo*, but that would've been incorrect. Max did *not* challenge the status quo. He had put himself in boxes all his life and refused to break out of them. Country boy. Blue-collar boy. Never-had-an-original-thought-between-his-ears-and-liked-it-that-way boy. Max's political opinions were primarily a regurgitation of his parents' backwater views, only slightly—and *slightly*—more empathetic to minorities. Being with Paula was, twistedly, the most progressive thing he had done his entire life.

And yet, Paula was clearly too fucked in the head for Lou to ever consider supporting them. His woe-is-me tactics back at the restaurant made her think twice, yes, but now this was evidence of a mental disorder, some kind of descent into a complete breakdown. Paula had gone from being a self-centered, abusive hippie to a sex fiend with a death fetish. The last thing Max needed to worry about was marrying her.

She reached for her luggage, gripping onto the handle. Max sighed.

"You said you'd give this a shot."

"I did."

She moved for the door, but as she was about to exit, the door swung open and a slight woman entered. The familiar wrinkles on her face had only deepened in the ten years since Lou last saw her. The blue eyes that matched hers, once so bright and piercing, were now somewhat milky, symptomatic of baby cataracts beginning to grow. Directionless wisps and tendrils of icy white hair, matted in some parts, clustered around her oddly small head. Her gloved hands were smeared with dirt, one clenched around a garden trowel, its scratched silver tip nearly obscured by mud. Lou remained silent, transfixed, as if unsure of what to say.

"Hey there, stranger," Paula chuckled, reaching out to try and give her a hug. Lou shrank back, but the older woman enveloped her, squeezing her with enough force to crack a couple of the joints in her back. "Look how you've grown."

Lou pushed back, but the smile on Paula's face didn't evaporate. She looked between Paula and Max, whose eyes were now as big as moons.

Lou's voice shook in its conviction as she spoke. "I was on my way out."

"Out?" Paula asked, her voice sounding far-away. "But you just got here."

"Yeah, but I'm not staying." She gestured to the collection of taxidermy animals. "And I'm telling Dad about all of this."

Paula laughed, her dainty voice echoing through the hall. She almost sounded like an owl hooting in the dead of night. *Oh-hoo-hoo-hoo. Oh-hoo-hoo-hoo.* A seemingly harmless sound that sent a chill down Lou's spine nonetheless.

"And what would you be telling him?" Paula asked, crossing her arms. "Max, did you tell her I do taxidermy as a side business?"

"I did," Max said. He looked to Lou, eyes pleading. "Maybe we could put some of them away, if that makes you more comfortable."

"We'll do no such thing. She's a guest in our home," Paula said. "A guest doesn't get to dictate the decor."

"I'm not—Paula, I'm *not* staying here."

"Paula?" A watchful finger scolded her. "Careful."

"Grandma," Lou corrected. "I'm not staying here. I only came because I wanted to figure out what was going on."

"Figure out what was going on?"

"I needed to make sure you weren't being taken advantage of."

Max interjected, "She was worried about you."

"Worried?" That uncomfortable smile returned to Paula's face. "That's interesting. You were worried about me? That's what motivated you to come out here after years of radio silence?"

"Yes."

"Why? Worried he might cut into your inheritance?" Paula nodded toward Max, who shrank into himself, looking like he wanted to melt into the tacky wildflower wallpaper surrounding them. "Because I can assure you, dear, there'll be nothing left once the burial's taken care of."

"Y-you can be taken advantage of in other ways. I was trying to make sure you aren't a victim of elder abuse or something."

"Why?" She shrugged in response. "It didn't concern you up until you received the invitation where I went, who I went with, and what I did."

"W-what are you even asking me? The invitation tipped me off. I had reason to suspect something bad was going down, so I came."

Paula smiled, glancing over at Max. "Hear that? She thinks you're suspicious."

"No! I mean, yes. But what's so wrong about that? If I think you're a victim or something, was I supposed to let you suffer? No. A good person wouldn't do that."

"Oh honey." Paula laughed. "There are no good people in this family."

Lou didn't feel any pain when the filthy trowel connected with her face.

FOUR

"IT WASN'T SUPPOSED TO HAPPEN like this."

Lou's eyes flickered open, but they were bleary, to the point where she couldn't see anything. All she knew was the world was dark, and it was a watercolor of muddy browns and blues and grays. The heat of the throbbing, damp pain in her left temple where Paula had struck her starkly contrasted with the cold she felt all around her. A tentative twitch of her finger communicated she lay on something smooth. Her aching head made it difficult to concentrate, but even so, she had no trouble understanding the harsh words exchanged between her captors.

"Why are you getting angry at me? If anything, I should be mad at you. You knew we needed her, and you were about to let her walk right out that door and back to the Cities. You had one job. You dilly dallied the whole afternoon. Damn it, what are we supposed to do? How are we going to get married at City Hall if we don't have a witness?"

"I-I can ask some of the guys at work."

"Your *coworkers*? Your filthy coworkers who don't even know how to wear a tie?"

"We have to figure something else out, honeybunch. For as much as I fucked up, least I didn't nearly debrain someone."

"You watch how you're talking to me, mister. I am your future wife. And *please*." Paula snorted. "I didn't debrain her. Mildly concussed her, maybe. But we can't damage her. We need her alive."

Shapes came into focus. Light entered from two different sources: a blistering overhead fluorescent lightbulb, and a mildew-glossed basement window with bars over it. Smooth concrete walls. The end of the stainless-steel table she was tied to. Was this their house or was she somewhere below it? She sucked in air through her nostrils, worried they'd overhear the sound of her shaky breaths rattling in her lungs. More to take in. An entire back wall full of shelves, lined with chemicals encased in plastic tubs and glass beakers. Jars shared the same space, their amorphous contents encased in some syrupy liquid. Lou squinted and saw small bodies of animals within them—tailless rats, infant guinea pigs, and wart-ridden toads—floating as though suspended by invisible string. A yellow toolbox ominously sat on a rolling cart in the back corner on top of a crimson-stained drain. But what was most concerning was the arsenal of cages and carriers stockpiled at the back of the room like some sort of demented jungle gym.

She was in deep shit.

Only her mother knew she was here to visit, but knowing her mom, the woman probably didn't remember when she said she'd be leaving or when she'd get back. Lou had two roommates, but they were the type of people to only care if she went missing when the Venmo notifications didn't pop up in their accounts on the first of the month. Until rent was due, they wouldn't care to figure out where she went.

She was on her own.

She wriggled, trying to see how tight her restraints were, but when she moved, she could feel bruises blossoming under her skin from where the ropes were pulled too tight. Voices echoed around her but no figures moved into her line of sight. She had no idea where Max and Paula were, but she knew she wasn't alone. Panic flooded her lungs like water submerging a broken submarine. Her breaths cracked like glass, harsh and sharp.

Lou glanced down at her wrist, and her heart somersaulted with joy when she saw her bracelet was still there. The chunky, corded rope bracelet was hideous and not worn for fashion purposes but for what was contained inside the buckle holding it together: a tiny blade sharp and pointed. She had gotten it at REI a few years ago when she had convinced herself she was going to start hiking more and had since held onto it for self-defense purposes. One of her restraints was looser on the left side, so she began to contort and twist her hand trying to wriggle it out. If she could loosen up this hand and get hold of her bracelet, she could use it to cut away at the other ropes and break free.

As she worked on her task, she listened to Paula and Max's bickering. For a couple newly engaged, they sure sounded like they had been married for decades already.

Max's shaky voice echoed in her ears. "How are we sure this is going to work?"

"We've gotten this far, and *now* you're asking that question?"

A ferocious series of childish stomps followed, coming from directly above. *Ahh.* That's where they were. That meant she was currently in the basement or a cellar. Some cellar this was, though. Basements in Minnesota were supposed to be for extra fridges, moldy pool tables, maybe a laundry room—not a bizarro torture chamber Was this where Paula made her taxidermy masterpieces? How long had it taken them to build this? And why, why in God's name did it need to be *this* big of a space? What were they planning?

Miracles! Her hand was freed, and although her joints were cramping, she only had a few red marks to show for it. She wondered who had tied her up so carelessly. Had it been Max? She shook her head *Don't think about that right now.* She reached for her bracelet, snapped it off her wrist, and used the exposed blade to saw away at the ropes Her heart fluttered in her chest as she saw the blade slice away at the sinews. Occasionally, she nicked herself, but it didn't hurt worse than a papercut would. Blood dribbled from the small wounds, soaking the musty brown fibers. God, this place smelled *awful.* She hadn't realized until now how bad it was. Chemical-laden, like someone had poured bleach all over the floor. It made her head throb harder as she worked, but she gritted her teeth, pushing through.

Once her other hand was free, she was able to work on untying her legs. Max and Paula's arguing continued to grow louder above her. She rolled her eyes, cheeks burning in anger. Max had gaslit the shit out of her, but she didn't know why she had let him do it. She knew Paula wasn't all right in the head. She had never been. Why had she let his words get in her head? Why had she ever felt guilty about this? She left this town and them behind for a reason. She came here to rescue Paula as though she was a lost little lamb, only to realize she had thrown herself into the lion's den.

Stupid, stupid, stupid.

Legs now free, she wiggled the ropes off her ankles, and they fell to the floor with a hearty *THUMP*. She sat up on the table and jumped off, staggering on the landing, the table collapsing beside her with a loud crash. She froze, eyes wide. *Shit.* She thought it had been screwed into the floor; it had barely moved when she was working her way out of the restraints. Had they heard that?

Echoes of footsteps thudding against the ceiling warned her they had. Whimpering, Lou clutched onto her pathetic bracelet and scanned the room for anything to serve as a better weapon. Bottles and bottles of chemicals spoke to her in languages she didn't understand. She could smash a beaker or a test tube but was that much better than the little bracelet she had?

Sounds of a squeaky door reverberated through the air. Yes, yes, anything was better than this piss-poor excuse of a knife. After dropping the bracelet, she reached for the largest beaker she could find on the shelf and smashed it against the end of a counter. It took a few good strikes, but finally it shattered, glass sprinkling onto the floor like confetti from a piñata. Oh, they were going to have a party down here, alright. Lou would make sure of it.

Max was the first to enter the doorway, his nostrils flared like a bull's, but his eyes were wide like a child's. Lou pointed the glass object in his direction, jutting it back and forth like a master fencer inviting her opponent to a duel. He took a step back. His eyes darted to what she could only assume was the entrance to the dwelling. The sound of slippers shuffling against pavement continued down the hallway behind him.

"Is she free?" Paula croaked, to which Max nodded, and like a banshee from hell, screeched, "Then *do* something!"

"She's armed," Max replied, pointing at her.

Paula appeared in the doorway. Gone were the dirty gardening clothes, and in their place, a paisley sleeved muumuu with a scooped neckline sloping across her shoulders, which were partially obscured by the waterfall of hair trailing over them. Her sequined sandals glittered like disco balls in the light. She looked like she was ready to go to a happy hour. She had bludgeoned her only grandchild, and yet—

"Louella," Paula snapped, eyes squinted into thin lines with disapproval. "You stop this foolishness right now."

Lou's laughter came out in high-pitched shrieks that would make a howler monkey blush. Loud, ringing, capable of traveling great distances, except they were stuck here in this damned basement, so it only bounced off the walls. Max winced and plugged his ears.

"You're going to let me out of here right now," Lou snapped. Her anger felt so righteous, so electrifying all the hairs on her body bristled. "Before I do something you'll regret."

"Lou—" Max said, his voice soft, but Paula held up a hand, silencing him.

Her muumuu swished from side to side as she approached Lou. Lou shouted at her wordlessly, her voice guttural, a cavewoman facing off against an ancient beast. Paula didn't flinch. A hurt expression crossed her face, and she rubbed the parchment paper skin along her hands and wrists.

"Fuck you and your pouty-ass face," Lou yelled, and God, it felt so good to yell at this monster of a narcissist. "You're going to let me go!"

"Am I?" Paula asked.

"Or I'll—I'll—"

"If you're going to do it, you should do it." Paula chuckled, shaking her head. "You haven't changed a bit. All talk and no action."

"Fuck you!"

Lou screeched, and with that, she raised the weapon over her head, preparing to strike Paula with it. Time slowed at this moment, and she wondered, curiously, why wasn't Max intervening? Was he going to watch as she struck Paula in the face? But then she heard it, from the din of the darkness. A high pitched, buzzing sound she couldn't place. Fingers—no, *claws*, sharp ones, scraped against her scalp, and with a shriek, she twisted around to swipe at the attacker, only to find herself staring face to face with a creature unlike anything she had ever seen before.

FIVE

IT WAS A BAT. OR AT some point, it had been a bat. Gone were its piglike nose and beady black eyes. In fact, the only thing that made her certain it *had* been a bat were its large, mouse-like ears shaped like saucers and its massive wingspan. It had the tail of a rabbit, white and fluffy, and its eyes were borrowed from a cat's. Up close, she could see its Frankensteined body, sewn together with tattered bits of flesh. Not even the chemical smell of this place could cover up the creature's rancid odor, of rot and feces and matted fur.

Lou shrieked, smacking it straight across the face with a broken beaker. A spurt of blood gushed out before it collapsed to the floor in a defeated heap, along with the rest of the glass, which shattered. Horrified, she watched as the monster bled out on the floor. Paula released a bloated wail that shook the walls of the room.

"Not Gregor!"

Max strode over to Lou and wrapped his arms around her waist, the veins in his muscles bulging. Lou screamed, thrashing back and forth in his vice-like grip. She tried to kick Max's knee but couldn't get the leverage to do so. Hovering over the crumpled body of the creature, Lou saw more things in the darkness. Glass containers full of formaldehyde housed creatures crafted with snarling animal faces and multicolor pelts like a fucked up version of Joseph's dreamcoat. Some were taxidermy and tacked to the walls. Cats' heads on dogs' bodies and birds of prey with antlers stuck to their heads with bits of coagulated blood.

They were all dead.

"Lou! Would you calm down? You're only making it worse!"

The filthiest of obscenities flew from Lou's mouth, along with droplets of spittle. Paula migrated to the yellow toolbox, reached inside, and withdrew a syringe. She popped off its cap, exposing the sharp needle beneath, and grabbed a small bottle of liquid from the shelf. She loaded the syringe with the liquid, then walked back over.

"Hold her steady," she said to Max, and he grunted in response. "This will help you relax a bit."

"What the fuck is that?" Lou aimed her foot at Paula's shin, but she skirted away from her in time.

"A little something I've concocted. Don't worry, it's non-addictive."

Lou's eagle screech emptied her lungs. Max's arms crushed against her rib cage. It took Paula no time at all to find an exposed vein and jam the needle into her skin. The pain that followed was swift and harsh, like a balloon on the verge of bursting. Paula held up the syringe, now emptied of liquid.

"All done." A smile teased across her leathery lips. "Let her go, Max."

"Isn't she—"

Paula giggled. "Come on, let her go."

Max released his grip, and for the briefest of moments, Lou felt sweet relief. It swelled within her chest, lifting her upwards. She took a step forward and her legs buckled like a Jenga tower with the structural pieces removed. She crumpled to the floor beside the animal's corpse, and Paula cackled. Max did not laugh. Lou's body turned to Jell-O against the cool concrete, her buttery limbs unable to apply the necessary pressure to lift herself up. The bizarre sensations—or lack thereof—which swept through her body were unlike anything she had ever experienced.

Paula continued to laugh, mocking her as she gestured for Max to reset the knocked-over table. "I know you don't like it, but you left me with no choice, dearie."

"Paula."

"Can't you let me have a little fun?"

"Cruelty and having fun aren't the same thing, sweetcheeks."

Despite his protests, Paula ignored him and crouched beside Lou. She lifted one of her wrists and allowed it to splat against the ground. It hurt Lou somewhat, but the sensation was dulled. Another raucous giggle escaped.

"Oh, this is good. This is very, very good."

"What are we wasting time for? Come on," he begged. "Please."

"Hey," she snapped again. "I'm not the one who screwed up here, babycakes. My plan was simple. She was going to be our witness, and *then* we would bring her down here. You're the dumbass that decided to bring her back to our house."

"She wanted to stay here. Said she wanted to avoid shelling out big money for the weekend."

"I don't care. That wasn't part of the plan."

Panic fluttered in Lou's chest and sweat began to seep out of her pores. In the brief texting conversations they had before she drove up, Max had invited her to stay at the house with them, and that was when he also asked to meet her at the diner. Why had he done that if he wasn't supposed to do it in the first place? And why was he lying to Paula now?

Max peeled Lou's sweaty body off the floor like excess glue from a children's art project, and draped her across the table. As he redid her restraints, he gazed at her pitifully, brown eyes remorseful.

"M-maybe if we've deviated from the plan so much," he said, "we shouldn't stick to it."

"Did you not see what she did? She killed Gregor. One of my firsts. He's not dying for nothing."

Gregor . . . the creature? Paula made that thing? How? Judging from the smell, and the menagerie of animals that occupied every space of this hellhole, it seemed like Paula was spending her days building Frankenstein's. Her whole life she had wondered why her grandmother, selfish demon that she was, had ever been a veterinarian. She didn't like people, and she didn't own a single pet. Was her interest in medicine purely related to experimentation? Maybe that was it. Maybe Paula knew she couldn't carry out these nature-defying surgical adventures with humans—too risky.

But animals could not advocate for themselves.

Lou's brain, befuddled with drugs and still fuzzy from her injury, struggled to put bits and pieces of this plan together. A concrete basement—probably soundproof—in a house on the outskirts of nowhere. A bizarre animalistic experiment. A desperation to have her *Her.* Not just her presence . . .

Oh God. What was going on?

"Okay, sweetheart," Paula hummed, "let me explain what's happening here, since I'm sure you're confused. I need your body. *We* need your body."

"What . . ."

Her lips were too parched to form full sentences and her tongue felt bloated and sticky, like a used super-size tampon. She attempted to wet her lips, and Paula giggled at her uselessness. Inwardly, Lou burned with shame. She had never been *this* high before, not even that night at First Ave when she had smoked an entire bowl on top of six shots of tequila. If her body wasn't so numb, she would be throwing up right now from the dizziness.

"Don't hurt yourself, kiddo. So." Paula drummed her fingertips against the tabletop. "You never knew your grandfather. William. Grandpa Willy. Whatever."

"Does she need to know this?"

"Hush, honey." Paula leaned in closer to Lou's face. Hot breath puffed against her nose and eyes, making them water. She smelled of minty denture paste and something rancid. Possibly a rotten tooth at the back of her mouth. "You couldn't fathom how fabulous I was before I got married. My life was *The Mary Tyler Moore Show*. Ambitious young career woman with my own practice, but so insecure. So desperate for someone to love me.

"And he was *such* a charmer. Swept me off my feet when I was a dumb little slut not much younger than yourself. I wanted to get my rocks off. I knew I was getting too old to get a man to do it." She paused to look at Max. "Least, that's what I thought, until this angel came along." Paula flashed a lovestruck grin at Max before returning to her story. "Well, I married William. And then I fucking hated William. And then William hated me so much he fucked me over so I couldn't leave him. And then I had your father, and let me tell you, Lou, a bit of your soul dies when you have a child with a man you hate. A child you didn't even want."

Lou hadn't known much about her late grandfather, but her curiosity got the better of her as a child when she realized, as opposed to her other friends' families who had sprawling albums filled with photos of their relatives, those sentimental items were absent from their home. Once, while rummaging through the drawers of Paula's desk, she found wilted parcels with printed images that spanned across the decades. Inside were photos of her father playing in a field as a child, and of her grandmother lounging on a pontoon floating on a lake. The photographs were keys to her distant past, but they couldn't answer why her grandfather wasn't present. When she had been found out (and screamed at by Paula) she had asked her parents about him. The anxious glances and profound silence that followed communicated he was not a good person. She didn't need Paula to tell her these things in order to understand that.

"I . . ." Lou whispered, gulping down air. Her throat was beginning to moisten again, little by little. "I don't . . . understand."

Paula giggled. She pressed her finger into Lou's head-wound, enunciating every word. "And! You! Won't!" She shrugged her shoulders. "You won't. God bless your little lesbian soul. 'Bout the only thing I ever liked about you." A deep breath. "Three decades of suffering ended when he died from a coronary. His skinny little ass always liked burgers. Made *me* diet because I was such a goddamn moo-cow, but *LOOK WHO'S THRIVING NOW, FUCKER!*"

She threw back her head and howled at the ceiling, and Max smiled, enamored. Waves of nausea rocked Lou's stomach. *No, Max.* She thought. *Don't pity her.* Paula always played the victim. Second to being a vet, it was what she was best at.

"I resigned myself to a life without love," Paula whispered, caressing Lou's face. "I thought I'd never experience the magic of true love, until Maxie came along. And oh, let me tell you . . . the magic is real."

Lou wriggled uncomfortably. Sensation, tingling and red-hot like biting ants, crawled back into her limbs. She wasn't going to be down for much longer, but there was no way she could fight them both off and escape.

"And I thought to myself, what a waste. What a waste I didn't live the life of a wife and mother with a man I truly loved. Maxie here doesn't mind my body, but I do."

"Rockin' bod, babe."

"Thank you, darling. But I need yours, Lou. I need yours so I can live the life I've dreamed of." Paula spread her hands, gesturing to the space around them. "I took up studying taxidermy and applied my knowledge from being a veterinarian to this. To create a new life. To find a way to play God and defeat death."

"You call *that* creature back there 'new life'? It was a rotting, reanimated carcass."

"As long as it's breathing—which he was, until you so rudely killed him—it's a life."

"So what? You think that you can play with the laws of nature like that?"

Paula smiled. "I don't *think*. I know I can."

"But why?" Lou whispered. "Why do you need my body? Why can't you make your own?"

"Unlike the little creature you oh-so-meanly murdered, it's harder to put together a functional body from large cadavers. Tried to reanimate a moose." She scrunched up her face. "Didn't work out. Goes to shit after a matter of hours. So I can't dig up a dead body and make my own Barbie doll. I need a live one."

"But why me and not someone else?"

"Because my little cherub, if I used someone else . . ." She playfully booped her nose. "It wouldn't be *my* babies I'd be having, would it?"

"What?"

"I know your medical history. You grew up with me. You were raised, in part, by me. I know you're susceptible to high cholesterol, bouts of depression, and on your mom's side of the family, a fondness for alcoholism. But everyone else? They're a shot in the dark. Debilitating disorders are certainly a concern, but mostly, dumbass genes." She whipped around to face Max. "No offense meant, baby."

"None taken. You're brains and I'm brawn."

"The peanut butter to that sweet, sweet jelly of yours."

"Stop," Lou said, shuddering with disgust.

"Not to mention, you have my eyes. Aside from your nose and—well, dear, your abysmal hairline, I don't know what in the Sam Hill is going on there—you are the spitting image of who I was when I was younger. Which means I'll have babies, that more or less, look like me."

"So what?" Lou whispered, chuckling in disbelief. "What does this have to do with your experiments?"

"You remember the movie *Freaky Friday*, Lou?" Max asked.

"Darling . . ."

"Baby, if you try to explain it to her in that big-headed way of yours, she ain't gonna get it. Lou. *Freaky Friday*. Jamie Lee Curtis. We used to talk all the time about how hot Lindsay Lohan was in that movie, with her smoky eyes and skunky looking hair."

"Yes . . ."

"That's basically what Paula wants to do. She takes her brain—"

Paula shook her head, rubbing her temples. "*Not* my brain. My consciousness—"

"Right, her soul or whatever, and she puts it in your body."

"Then what happens to my consciousness?"

"We're going to put it in a cat."

Out of all the batshit things they had both said today, this, by far, was the worst of them.

Lou looked between them both, confused. "I'm sorry, just so I understand—"

"A cat. I can put you in the body of a cat until we find you a NEW body," Paula explained.

"Really," Lou said, unimpressed. "You sure you're not going to kill me?"

"No, no." Max waved his hands. "You won't die. We've got ways of tracking this. Well, Paula does, but it all goes far above my head. We'll know. There's tests we can perform to determine if the body swap worked."

"And when the fuck are you going to find me a new body?"

"Whenever," Paula responded. At the same time Max said in the cheeriest of tones, "Soon!"

The lovers glared and pointed an accusatory finger at each other.

"Talk about not part of the plan!" Max cried out in disbelief. "What do you mean, *whenever*? This is your granddaughter we're talking about! This is family!"

"Why do you always interpret everything I say in the worst way possible? Soon, whenever, what difference does it make?"

"Because we don't want to wait! What good is that going to do for her?"

"The sooner I get in her body, the sooner we can get up to no good."

"Paula, that's—that's straight up disrespectful to me. I'm sorry. I didn't agree to that."

"So you don't want me to do the transfer today?"

"No. Not without another body."

Paula froze, considering this. The palpitations in Lou's heart grew painful and ferocious, watching as anger surfaced in her grandmother's eyes. As soon as she spotted it, Paula blinked it away, batting her long, mascara-clumped eyelashes against her rouged cheeks. With a coquettish expression, she approached Max, her liver-spotted hands sliding along his arms. She pecked his lips, and he leaned into her embrace, the tension in his shoulders melting away.

"I suppose that's okay. If you wanted to, you could even test it out," she purred, sliding her hands along his shoulders.

Max's lips drew back in a confused snarl.

"You're going to have to get used to it," Paula said. "It *is* going to be my body after all. Besides, if we're gonna have kids, I'd rather we pop 'em out as soon as possible. She's . . . How old are you, Lou?"

Lou swallowed. "27."

"Right. Clock is ticking, or close to it."

"But she's not *you*," Max protested, concern seeping into his voice. He stared at Lou who was squirming on the examination table, too weak to fight against her restraints. "It'd be like—like cheating."

"Not if I'm giving you permission. And I don't want you to wait so long, darling. I know you've got your needs."

Her hand caressed his face, but she recoiled when he snatched her wrist.

"I'm not raping anyone, Paula," he said. "As long as she's still in that body, that's what it would be. You wouldn't want me to associate you with that now, would you?"

"N-no, my love," she replied, shock ruminating in her doe-like eyes.

"Once this is all over, dumpling, we'll fuck like rabbits." He released his grip on her wrist and pecked her forehead in a feeble apology. "We'll have a baby soon enough, don't you worry."

"You can't use me as some kind of incubator," Lou cried out. "It's *my* body! Not hers!"

"We'll get you an even better body. Paula can build one for you."

"Max," Lou said, voice giving way to sobs. "Please."

Dejected, he turned back to Paula, but she smiled and touched his shoulder.

"When we have a daughter, we'll name her after your sister. That's a promise. But we can't have a daughter until we have her body."

"Really!?" Lou screeched. "That is so fucking low, Paula!"

"It's *Grandma* Paula, you little shit!"

"Max, she's manipulating you!"

"I have had it with your disrespect!" Her eyes twitched ferociously. She removed a scalpel from the toolbox, waving it around.

"You want me to start this procedure right here, right now?"

"Whoa whoa whoa!" Max cried out, holding out a hand toward both women. "Paula, put that down! *Now*!"

Lou's chest heaved. She could barely think straight. How could she? Her grandmother and childhood best friend wanted to use her body so they could have a baby. So her grandmother could have a total do-over of her life and start anew. They were willing to kidnap and kill her to get what they wanted. There were few things in this world more fucked up than that.

And even fewer ways out of this situation.

In fact, there were no ways out of this situation.

Dread weighed her down. Even if she believed they could carry out this experiment successfully—which she did not believe they could—she would be doomed to spend the rest of her days as a cat until another hapless experiment could take place. In the tense silence, Lou ruminated on the hopelessness of her situation. What did people do when they were kidnapped? No. What did *smart* people do when they were kidnapped? They played along. They gained the trust of their captor. They gathered intel. They did whatever it would take to survive until they could escape or gain the upper hand.

"Let me pick out my body."

Max and Paula looked at her.

"Let me pick one out," Lou said. "And then I'll do it. It's the least you could do, since you're taking mine away from me."

"Paula?"

"You seriously . . ." Paula scoffed in disbelief. "She could just *not* agree to any body that we offer to put her in."

"We don't have to agree to this indefinitely. Only long enough for her to find a decent replacement. Something she can live in. Something the ladies will like," Max said to Lou with a grin, although she didn't smile back. "Come on, hon. She's right. We owe it to her."

"She owes me *her* life," Paula hissed, her eyes growing wet. "If it wasn't for me and the ways I suffered, she wouldn't even be here right now."

Max kissed her hands, giving them a tender squeeze. "You know what it's like to have your choices taken from you, darlin'. I'm asking that you don't take away the only one she's got left. Like she said, it's the least we can do."

Paula didn't respond, her hands limp within his grasp, staring at the floor as though her intense gaze could drill right through it. He coaxed her like a child.

"I know you're a better woman than this," he whispered. "Help me prove it."

SIX

WHEN LOU WOKE UP IN the basement, she had a fleeting thought she would never see the sun again. Words could not describe the awe-inspiring relief she experienced when they brought her up from the basement and she felt the last rays of dreamsicle sunlight on her face. But the moment itself was brief because, in the next, she was shoved into the back of Paula's VW bus. A foul stench assaulted her nostrils and she coughed, gagging on it. Earthy incense and the sour, rotten smell of the chewing tobacco Paula pretended not to use, along with something she now recognized as decayed flesh. With her wrists bound behind her back, she couldn't cover her mouth when she coughed, and her lungs sputtered violently as she breathed in the tarnished air. Her brain felt as though it was rattling around in her skull from the violent treatment and the aftereffects of the drugs, which made her heart feel heavy.

Then again, her heart could've been heavy from the dread.

With a soft smile, Max offered her a water bottle. Paula hadn't joined them in the van because she was still struggling to find her keys. Apparently she left this damn thing unlocked, which was another typical Paula thing to do. Lou found it strange that Max thought to grab her a fresh bottle from the fridge. He cracked it open and offered her a sip. Out of desperation, she accepted it, suckling on it like a newborn calf.

Once she had her fill, she wiped her mouth against her shoulder. "Nice of you to offer me a drink before I die."

"You're not gonna die. I won't let that happen."

"You're going to have a real hard time convincing me on that one. I mean, you let her hit me."

"I didn't know she was gonna do that. Surprised me as bad as it did you." His tone was even, steady. Eyes sympathetic. "She just wants another chance. If other people ruined your life, but you had a chance to redo it, wouldn't you take it? Heck, not even redo, but to be someone else?"

"Well, you're leaving me with no choice but to do that, so . . ."

"You've told me your whole life you don't like your face and you don't like your eyes. You never liked your hair much either, which is why you kept changing it. You don't think you'd jump for the chance to swap all those things out?"

"I have a better idea. Why don't *you* do a body swap, and then tell me how you feel?" She shook her head. "Stop trying to convince me this is what I actually want. You can gaslight me all you want, but I'm not gonna fall for it."

"I'm not trying to gaslight you."

"If you have to convince me to make the decision, then it's not *my* decision, is it? It's hers. And why you're letting her do all this, I don't—"

"Because I love her, Lou. And I want her to be happy. I love her and that's the only reason why I'd ever give this plan a lick of thought."

She stared at him. "That's not a good enough answer."

"And why not?"

"Are you fucking stupid, man? Did you not hear her whole thing about 'test the body' out?"

Guilt surfaced in his expression, making his eyes appear glassy. His voice left his throat in a mumble. "I don't think she meant that."

"Really? You don't think she meant it?"

"She's been through a lot of trauma. Traumatized people say and do fucked up things."

Lou was amazed at how Max could apply this logic toward Paula but not toward himself. Traumatized people also (apparently) slept with their childhood friend's grandmother and became accomplices to kidnapping and now potentially murder.

It didn't justify anything.

"I don't understand why you would want my body."

"Like Paula said, she wants someone who looks like her."

"Not Paula. *You.* Why would you want to be with *my* body?" Lou asked, aghast. "Are you attracted to me or something?"

Perhaps part of his motivation wasn't just to please Paula but to please himself and fulfill a wicked fantasy he had harbored all these years. Did he desire her? Even after she had come out to him? Was he truly so sick he had concocted an elaborate, devious scheme in order to be with her? She filtered through the memories but couldn't remember a time when Max had touched her inappropriately or came onto her. When he had visited her, he had slept on the couch without a complaint, and the weirdest thing he had done was sleep in a pair of briefs so short she could see the outline of his dick. But that seemed to be Max being Max. He could be sweet, but that didn't mean he was the most considerate person.

He shook his head. "No. I'm not."

"You're *sure* about that?"

"I'm not." He paused to consider this. "Like—maybe when we were in the second grade, I had a teeny tiny crush. But that was before Jessica Hartley's mom came along with her amazing rack."

"I fucking *knew* you had a thing for her."

"What can I say? I live for MILFs and GILFs. Least I'm consistent."

"But if it's not the same body you're attracted to, how is it going to work?"

Max picked at the dirt beneath his nails, his voice trembling a bit. "I'm not shallow. If it's her—if it's Paula in there—it'll be fine."

"'It'll be fine' isn't exactly reassuring now, is it?" Lou whispered, the words hot on her tongue like chili flakes. "Come on. You know I'm right. You're not going to be able to get it up. Not when you're thinking about me the entire time."

Max scowled. "Stop it."

Lou waggled her tongue. "See this? Eaten a *lot* of women out with this mouth. Imagine your tongue. Touching my tongue. And all those women's vaginas."

"*Lou.*"

Disgust ravaged his expression and his scowl grew bigger, yet in his eyes, there was something: horror. He was horrified by the idea of post-experiment life. Lou goaded him further.

"What? I'm just stating the obvious. Besides—I'm not only thinking about *you* and your ability to have fun. Think about what Paula's going to ask you to do. You think you're going to stick your head between my legs and—"

At that moment, Paula opened the door to the van.

SEVEN

MAX CLAMPED HIS MOUTH SHUT and smiled at Paula as she climbed inside. She planted her wilted lips against his cheek and slipped on her round sunglasses. She peered up in the rearview mirror and examined her teeth. Without speaking, she stretched out her hand, and Max rummaged inside the dashboard. He removed a floss stick from a little baggie and handed it to her. Disgusted, Lou watched as her grandmother proceeded to floss.

"Are we driving back into town?" Max asked. "I'm thinking scoping out The Thirsty Gopher would be great. Tons of bodies there. Drunk people are easy to kidnap."

"Good thinking," Paula replied. "Except we can't let her in there."

"Why not?"

"I don't trust her not to run." Paula glanced up at Lou in her rearview mirror. "She was always a runner as a kid."

"That's not true."

"It is. You broke that window at the old house, and you and your little friend took off running—"

"That *little friend* was Kelsea," Lou snapped. "Your soon-to-be-husband's sister."

"I don't remember that."

"Of course you don't."

Max looked between the two of them. "What?"

"Nothing. They broke a window." Paula waved a hand dismissively.

"Do you know what she did to Kelsea after she broke that window?"

"As I recall, I did it to *you*, not Kelsea."

"Well, you remember wrong." Lou turned to Max. "She hit her in the face with a baseball."

Max's eyes narrowed. "Paula, is that true?"

"No, it's not," Paula responded coolly. "The drug I gave her might be messing with her memory a little bit. The effects last a lot longer than you think they do."

From Paula's ferocious glare in the rearview mirror, Lou understood she had better not push it. She pressed her face against the streaked window. Out here there was nothing but cornfields and Trump lovin' farmers. She could find a way out of this situation if she played nice and got closer to town. From there she could plan her escape and get help. But pissing Paula off before the car started wasn't going to increase her chances of surviving whatever hellish nightmare she had been thrust into. And Max—the poor idiot—was letting himself be strung along by a woman who loved to play the victim.

Paula plucked the floss stick from between her teeth, rolled down the window, and dropped it outside. She adjusted her mirrors one last time before pressing down on the accelerator. Like most elderly people, Paula drove slow, painfully slow. Lou could see a tractor, far in the distance, cruising at a faster pace than they were. Max didn't seem to mind it though. He leaned out the window like a golden retriever, a wide smile across his face, arm resting against the rusted door. Miles and miles worth of corn, the exposed heads golden and shiny like doubloons, twinkled in the light of the late afternoon sun. The stalks that swayed in the breeze seemed to wave as they drifted by.

"So Lou," Max called out. Good God, the road noise was terrible. "What kind of body do you think you want?"

My own. "I don't know. Someone . . . fit. Around my age. That would be a good place to start."

In this town, that had to be a tough thing to find. People out here lived off pale ales, cheese curds, and stuffed burgers fresh off a greasy grill. But Paula took this feedback in stride, nodding her head. Max scratched his beard.

"Uh, I mean, anything else?" He grinned and looked over at Paula. "Like, if I was going to change bodies—"

"You're perfect the way you are, sugar—"

"I know, I know, but if I *was*, you know what'd I do? Be a muscle man. *Oh*. Or I'd be a girl with big bazongas. Honking bazongas like yours, babe. I'd jump up and down, go for a run, feel 'em up, really get an idea for what it's like."

"The tiny titty community will be sorry to disappoint you," Lou grumbled underneath her breath. Her chest had been as flat and square as a ream of paper for as long as she could remember. Not that she minded it too much. She looked damn good in a button-down shirt.

"No need to worry about that," Paula said to Max. "Pregnancy makes your breasts fill out."

Lou pictured her not-self standing in front of a full-length mirror, a naked belly so large her navel corkscrewed outward like a pig's tail, stretch marks forming a spider web across her skin. She envisioned Max's arms wrapped tightly behind her, his grizzled cheek nuzzling the nape of her neck as he planted a wet kiss, while her cat-self curled up in a loaf in the background. To think that was the good option—the option where she didn't die—disturbed her. Lost in her haunted reverie, she almost didn't notice when they drove past the hiker on the side of the road, blond ponytail fluttering in the wind like a white flag.

Paula slammed on the brakes, ramming Lou into the back of the driver's seat, and Max braced himself against the dash, alarmed. Lou was surprised he hadn't screamed. Ghostly-white, he turned to look at Paula, but her eyes didn't meet his. She threw the car into reverse and accelerated backward, screeching to a halt beside the woman.

Lou peered out the passenger window, but it was hard to see through the tinted glass. The hiker was at best in her mid 20s. Crew length socks inched their way up her pronounced calves. Her knees were scuffed up and dirty, as though she had taken a bad fall. In one hand she gripped a walking stick carved from a broken birch branch. She stared at the van with a displeased expression, top lip curled upwards in a scowl. Her eyes were hidden behind a pair of oversized aviators.

"Paula?" Max whispered, glancing over at his bride.

"Make nice, Maxie." She rolled down the window.

"H-hey there!" Max tried to sound cheery, but it was obvious he was nervous. "You're a long way from town."

The girl laughed, shrugging her shoulders. "Yeah, I think I missed the trail a while back."

"Trail?"

"Uh-huh. Paul Bunyan Park?"

"Shoot, girl, you're a ways away from where you need to be. How'd you end up all the way out here?"

Paula drummed her fingertips against the steering wheel, lips pressed together so tightly they were almost nonexistent. She nudged Max and he stammered again. "Uh, well, we could give you a ride over there, if you'd like. We were on our way back into town. Might as well."

Perhaps the girl's survival instincts kicked in, because she frowned and shook her head. The polite smile remained plastered across her face. "That's okay."

She started to walk away, and for the briefest of moments, Lou released a sigh of relief.

Tktktktk.

Eyes widened as she saw her grandmother's nails click against the steering wheel. Grimacing, Paula reversed the van again, tires grinding against the road with a ferocity that frightened Lou and Max. The hitchhiker, perplexed, stood there, but it wasn't until the van rolled in front of her she realized what was happening. She screamed and turned to run into the corn stalks, but Paula gunned it, engine screeching in protest. The thud that followed was sickening, and as they drove over her body, Lou could feel it crunching underneath the belly of the van. Corn stalks crumpled against the windshield and hood of the van as they stopped a few inches inside the plot.

Max remained frozen, jaw clamped shut, air fleeing his nostrils in audible whistles. Unbothered, Paula threw the van into park, then looked at Lou.

"Don't think I damaged her too much. Want to hop out and take a look?"

"I don't . . ."

Lou trembled violently, deep in shock. She hadn't assumed her grandmother was going to kill some random stranger. Kidnap her, yes, but she didn't think she'd be so eager to cause bodily harm. Had this actually happened, or was the drug in her system making her hallucinate? But if it didn't *really* happen, why was Max freaked out?

"You don't what?" Paula snapped.

"Did you kill her?"

Barely audible moans, grievous and wet, communicated that was *not* the case.

"She'll be fine. I've got ways of fixing her up."

"Paula, I don't—"

"Get the fuck out of my van, Lou."

Lou held up her bound wrists with a thin, shaky smile. Paula rolled her eyes and pushed open her door before cracking open the back door of the van. Fingers as hot as branding irons dug into Lou's arms and she was tugged from the van with a surprising strength. The sounds of the girl's moans grew louder in volume, and Lou squeezed her eyes shut, terrified.

"Don't do that." Paula slapped her in the face, just enough to make her open her eyes again. "I did all this for you, and you can't be bothered to look at it?"

Gone was the hitchhiker's smooth, perfect ponytail. It was ratty now, matted with dirt and blood. Parts of her scalp appeared to have peeled off her skull, exposing the raw membranes and stretchy adipose fibers arranged in a mesmerizing pattern beneath. It reminded Lou of salmon sashimi. The girl's face was a bloodied mess, marred by metallic bits and blackened pieces from her shattered sunglasses. Her limbs were twisted in opposite directions, and her body scrunched at her abdomen like an accordion. Slack-jawed, her heavy eyes fluttered as she stared up at them, and Lou couldn't help but notice her irises were blue.

"I don't want her," Lou whispered.

"Excuse me?"

"I don't want her," Lou repeated. "She's . . . she doesn't fit the criteria."

"You said athletic and around your age."

"I said those were the qualities I wanted to start with. I-it was my baseline," Lou stammered. The sounds of the girl's breathing, constricted by the phlegm and blood bubbling up within her lungs, made it difficult to concentrate. Lou shook her head over and over again. "I wanted—I didn't—I didn't want this. I didn't want her. You decided on her for me."

A spark ignited within Paula's eyes, and she clenched her jaw. "And what would make you happy, Louella? I nearly kill this girl for you, and that's not good enough?"

"Paula," Max's tired voice echoed from inside the van.

"No," Paula shouted back. Tears burned her blistered blue eyes. She shook a finger at Louella, scolding her as if she was a child. Hell, Lou thought, she probably still saw her as one. "I tell you how much of my life I've spent suffering, and you want to make me jump through hoops to get my happiness? What kind of narcissistic monster are you?"

Max stumbled out of the van, slamming the door shut behind him. "Paula—"

"No!" she squealed, stomping her foot on the ground. "This was supposed to be *my* wedding! My big day! And instead of other people making my dreams come true, I'm running around committing vehicular manslaughter for my selfish bitch of a granddaughter!"

"It's not vehicular manslaughter," Lou mumbled.

"What?"

"She's still alive. So technically not vehicular manslaughter."

Max reached out to comfort Paula, but she shoved him away and climbed back into the driver's seat. Max squeezed the sides of his head, eyes fixed to burst, as he watched her start the van again, ignition coughing up blood, and throw it in reverse.

"You fuckers want vehicular manslaughter? I'll *show* you vehicular manslaughter!"

Max grabbed hold of Lou and tugged her away from the van just as the back tires crunched over the injured girl. One rear tire slid backward over the top of her skull and ripped off the rest of her scalp and hair, exposing the pomegranate seed brains beneath. On impact, her jaw sprung forward on her lopsided tongue, snapping it in two and leaving the lump of flesh to wriggle on the ground, a fish out of water. The other tire crunched over her hip bone, shoving it deep into her body, pulverizing the organs within her pelvic region. Blood pooled out from every exposed orifice and Lou could only watch, mesmerized with fear, as some of the droplets splattered against her face.

Although he was shaking, Max didn't release Lou from his embrace. Wide-eyed, he stared at Paula, who was now slumped over the front of the steering wheel, exhausted. His parted mouth opened to speak to her, but as soon as it did, she flipped the van into drive, moved forward, and reversed it again. Over and over, she drove across the top of the body until it was pulpy like the insides of a red pumpkin. This time, Max had the good sense to turn Lou's head away from the horror of it all. With her face pressed against his plaid shirt, she allowed herself to cry for the first time that day. This was the first murder she had witnessed, but not the first death, and the way he held her felt painfully familiar.

EIGHT

BY THE TIME PAULA FINISHED driving over the corpse, it resembled the goo at the bottom of a tube of toothpaste. Blood was splattered all over the front of the van and dripped from its undercarriage like an open wound, yet miraculously, it hadn't broken down and the tires were still intact. Satisfied with her handiwork, Paula turned off the van and exited, looking between the shaken best friends.

"What?" she asked. "Did you want to get caught?"

"How are you not going to get caught?" Lou demanded.

"Please. When the farmer sees this, he'll think it was a deer." Paula nudged a bit of blubber with the tip of her boot. "Semis blow through here on occasion. Ain't strange to see a carcass that looks like this."

"What about her stuff?"

"We're taking it. Any more dumbass questions you'd care to ask?" Paula hissed, and when Lou was silent, her eyes flitted to Max. He hadn't let go of Lou this whole time. Paula appraised their fear in disbelief. One hand reached up to fumble with the chain of her necklace, wringing it between her fingers. Her ice cold stare chilled them but offered no reprieve from the heat.

"Get back in the van."

Obediently, they retreated to the vehicle and Paula loaded the dead girl's belongings into the back. It took her far longer than it should have, but neither of them questioned it. There was nowhere else for them to go unless they wanted to play tag in a cornfield, and with her hands bound this tight, Lou didn't like her chances. Paula started the van once more and peeled off for home, mumbling something about needing to clean off all the blood, the smell of which filled Lou's nostrils with a nauseating pungency. Some of the blood had soaked through the girl's backpack and coated the walking stick, and now, as they drove along the unsteady road, it was smearing around on the floorboard. Lou grimaced and, with a trembling foot, pushed the backpack to the opposite wall of the vehicle, attempting to keep it as far from her as possible.

Seeing that Max was silent, Paula rolled down the window, as if to encourage him to lean outside yet again. But unfortunately her golden retriever lover didn't bite. He shook his head, his eyes staring into oblivion.

Fingernails drummed against the steering wheel, and Lou's heart hitched in her throat as she heard her grandmother's voice. "Are we going to have a problem here, shmoopie?"

"N-no," Max stammered at first, but then his eyes narrowed. "Actually—"

"*Actually* what, Maxwell?"

"Bunny, I knew that to get what we wanted, it wasn't going to be pretty. But this time you've gone way too far."

"What?"

"No one was supposed to die. We killed that little girl back there."

"Little girl?" Paula repeated, the growls ripping from her throat. "Little girl? Since when did you care about a little girl? The only one you should be caring about is me!"

"I do, honey, I just—"

"And I'm sorry, 'we'? *We* did not kill her back there. I did. Unless you're willing to get thrown in the slammer over what happened. Take the fall. Like a good man would."

Max stared back at her coldly. His jaw set in a firm line. It was as if he finally understood, for the first time, how crazy this woman was.

"You're not well, honey," he whispered. "Pull over and give me the keys. Let me drive. You need to get some rest."

Paula banged her fists against the steering wheel like a toddler throwing a tantrum, wailing wordlessly. The van swerved from side to side and Lou belched as the contents of her mediocre lunch bubbled inside her. Max's hands reached across with lightning precision, grabbing the steering wheel and correcting their course before they crashed into yet another cornfield. Mascara tears streamed down Paula's face, and her sunglasses slipped down the bridge of her nose. Beneath her, Lou could feel the van vibrating with a vicious intensity, a prowling cougar about to pounce on its prey. She watched as the arrow on the speedometer pushed up, up, up . . .

"Paula, you *have* to steer—"

"You don't want to marry me any-*more-ah*!" she howled.

He raised his voice. "You're wrong! I do! I still do!"

The speedometer's needle descended. Paula sniffled, pushing her hand against her snotty nose as if to blow it. Thin webs of mucus stretched between her face and her open palm, and she held it in the air for some reason. Did she not want to touch the steering wheel again or was she asking for Max to hold her hand? As they sped along, Lou watched as her sobbing grandmother turned to look at Max, her breaths hitching in her throat, her eyes slowly narrowing into laser-thin slits.

His eyes betrayed the words he spoke.

And Paula knew it.

With a scream, her slimy hand snapped forward and entangled in the back of his hair. Max didn't even have time to react and, unfortunately for him, he hadn't put on his seatbelt. She slammed his head against the dashboard three times. Shrill sobs escaped Lou's lips as Paula finally released him. He didn't move, but blood dripped from his ear.

"Shut up!" Paula screeched, pressing down on the accelerator again. "Or I'll do it! I swear to God I'll do it! I'll crash this fucking van into that field, and the birds can peck the eyes out of your corpse!"

To stifle her sobs, Lou buried her face against her shoulder. Her shirt smelled like Max. She never thought she would find his gross musk comforting. Now it was the only thing that could save her from the overwhelming odor of pennies. She squeezed her eyes shut, trying to ignore the sound of the roaring engine. The van bumped along, and she braced herself as she slid across the slippery, blood-covered floor. It felt like she was inside a pinball machine. Pain erupted in her shoulder when Paula drove around a particularly sharp corner. All the while, she studied Max's slumped body. Relieved sobs bubbled up in the back of her throat when she realized, yes, he was still breathing.

Still breathing, but probably wouldn't wake up anytime soon.

Through the windows, the house loomed closer. The van screeched to a halt and she was thrown against the driver's seat one last time. Paula groaned in agony as though she had been injured the most.

"First thing we're going to do, we're going to lose some weight. Yes, we are," Paula grumbled as she climbed out. "By the time I'm finished with you, you'll be as big as a baby bird."

"Grandma," Lou begged, her voice hoarse. "Please let me go. I won't tell anyone—"

"*Myeh, myeh, myeh.* 'I won't tell anyone, Grandma.' 'I promise, Grandma.' 'I swear on my life, Grandma.' You aren't five anymore, Lou. This shit ain't cute, if it ever was to begin with." Paula whipped open the side door, dragging her out by the ear and throwing her onto the gravel driveway. Lou winced as the gritty asphalt scraped and ground against her face like a pumice stone. "Actually, I never found it cute. Neither you or that selfish sunnabitch you call your father. Speaking of which, why didn't he come to see me?"

"Why didn't—what? Because you didn't send him an invitation."

"I did. I sent him an invitation."

Lou stared at her, perplexed. Max told her she was the only one who had been invited. Had her father actually received an invitation or was she misremembering? She wasn't close to her dad—didn't even talk to him on a birthdays-and-holidays basis—but would he have really not mentioned anything? Would he have not gone out to help his elderly mother and figure out what the fuck was going on?

Had he allowed her to suffer alone?

"Selfish, selfish, selfish." Paula clicked her tongue against her tobacco-stained teeth. "Your dad is as bad as his father was. And like father, like daughter, Louella. You're a controlling little pissant who never respected my authority. If you had cooperated with me, I wouldn't have had to do that to my future husband."

Lou looked toward the van, hoping to see Max stirring in the passenger seat. But before she could register whether he was moving or not, Paula grabbed her chin, squishing her cheeks as close together as she could. Spittle bubbled up between Lou's swollen lips as she gazed back at Paula's wild eyes. Wild eyes, wild hair, wild as the hills she roamed. Nothing about her grandmother had ever been tame, and now that Lou was in this situation, she didn't know why she had assumed she would be.

Shik. The sound of switchblade being released echoed through the air. Light refracted off the surface of the switchblade, shining into Lou's eyes. Her heartbeat quickened, and little black spots danced within her field of vision. She noticed the blood that was already on it, along with a suspicious sliver of skin with small squiggles on it, like a cross section of a tree. It took her a moment to realize it was a fingerprint. Paula had removed the fingerprints from the corpse. No wonder it had taken so long for her to put the girl's things in the back of the van.

Paula rubbed her thumb across the blade, flicking away the flesh like it was nothing more than a flea. Then she scraped the blade across Lou's skin, carving a small half-moon onto the surface of her cheek. Lou's eyes watered and she held her breath, strangling the scream rising within her throat. Paula arched her brow.

"You're going to tell me exactly what I need to know." Her thumb swiped away the blood again. "Or I'll skin you like a rabbit. Choice is yours."

"Tell you what?" Lou sobbed.

"Out of courtesy to my fiancé, I'm going to give you one last shot to make this decision for yourself. Who do you want to be? Because you're no granddaughter of mine." Paula pricked her skin with the blade. "You're going to pick your new body, and when you wake up in it, you are going to be *so* happy you'll convince Max he still wants this. Do you understand me?"

Max. Lou felt her heart thump against her chest. He had gotten her into this mess, and he probably deserved to burn for it, too. But out of respect to Kelsea and the blood promise they had made as children, she would not forsake him. He had stumbled, he had lost his way. Maybe part of that was her fault, maybe it wasn't. But he had promised her he wouldn't let her die, so she would do the same for him. She had already buried one best friend. She didn't want to bury two.

Lou's lungs squeezed in desperation as she pushed words through her squished-tunnel lips. "I . . ."

Paula lowered her blade. "Yes?"

"I'll . . . tell you," she gasped. Within the seconds that followed, her brain performed a tremendous number of calculations, numbers tumbling over the top of each other in her head in a complicated dance of multiplication and division. She had to make a *good* decision. One that wasn't impossible, but could buy her enough time to get help. "M-muscular, like before. Not a beefcake, though. U-u-uh, natural blond hair. And I want brown eyes."

"*Brown*?"

"If I'm going to be forced to start over, I-I want to look completely different," Lou whispered, gulping down air between every few words. "And sever my ties to you."

To Paula, to this cursed family that never spoke to one another, to this entire goddamn town that had left Max alone to stew in his silence and grief. She knew the dig was harsh, and she winced, bracing for impact, but Paula merely chuckled in response, amused.

"I think I know of just the gal."

NINE

TOO FRUSTRATED TO CLEAN THE blood off her van, Paula retrieved the keys to Max's truck from the house and pulled it around front. Though Lou could've run, she chose not to since, again, her wrists were tied and she'd have to chance making her way through the maze of cornstalks and fighting back against her homicidal grandmother. Plus, that would have meant leaving Max behind. He still hadn't woken up, and in his slumber, Paula had taken the opportunity to bind his wrists and ankles. She cracked the windows of the van but left him inside.

"Couldn't he die in the heat?" Lou whispered.

"That's why the windows are down." Ice water eyes pierced through her with malice. "And I don't remember asking you for your goddamn opinion. Get your ass in the truck."

As Lou scrambled into the passenger's seat, she squeezed her eyes shut, trying to figure out what to do next. She needed to convince Paula to let her talk to whoever this next victim was. Clearly, from how Max had helped her earlier, the woman wasn't too hard to persuade, as long as you made her think it was her idea, or that it would make her look better. But as the truck headed down the driveway, Lou's body filled with dread. They were leaving behind the only person who could help her if things went south.

As they rolled down the road, she remained silent, trying to distract herself by examining the little trinkets Max had stowed away. A crocheted opossum suspended itself from the rearview mirror. Side door pockets were stuffed with tools, some of which were rusted, and a ton of receipts. The dash was cracked open, and inside she could see a driver's manual, gas station receipts, and an open box of condoms. *Oh. Great. That explains the stickiness of this seat.* Judging by the smell, this truck hadn't been cleaned since he bought it. A shame, too. It was a nice truck. Cherry red. When the three of them had to bike home after school, cursing the steep hill their houses sat on, Max had talked about getting a truck like this. A childhood dream achieved, and he didn't appreciate it enough to take proper care of it.

Yet he was confident he could spend the rest of his life taking care of Paula, even as she withered into madness.

When they breezed past the dead girl, Lou kept her eyes open, hoping to see some sort of cop car there, maybe even the farmer's tractor. But no one had discovered the goop-girl except a colony of overeager flies.

Paula noticed Lou's watchful gaze. "They won't figure it out."

"Someone'll be looking for her."

"You let me worry about that."

"Where are you taking me?"

"You'll see soon enough." Paula glanced over at her tied up hands. "Keep those on your lap. I don't want anyone seeing them. Remember I still got my knife on me."

Lou bit her lip. She watched as the rural prairielands bled away and the town came into focus. The truck made a few turns, and slowly, the roads became more familiar to Lou. There was the ice cream shop her friends had biked to every summer, now an insurance agent's office. Beside it, the abandoned Movie Gallery where they picked out movies every Saturday night. To her right, the mailbox Kelsea had got her arm stuck in one time when she changed her mind about sending a love letter to the boy she liked. Lou and Max had howled with laughter while she flailed about, arm clenched in the iron door. It took the two of them to wrench it down and set her free. Even though they eventually helped her, she slapped them over their cruel laughter.

"You stupid assholes!"

Kelsea didn't know how right she was when she called them that.

After stopping at a traffic light, the truck made another turn, this time, headed further away from the direction of town. Lou's heart crawled up the back of her throat, but Paula appeared emotionless. Lou mouthed the street names as they passed, each one triggering her memory, but it wasn't until they drifted around a sharp corner she realized, finally, where they were heading.

Paula's old veterinary practice.

It was a simple one-story brick building, industrial and isolated. When Lou was a child there had been a gas station down the road from here, but that had since closed. Its windows boarded up and a leasing sign stuck in the scraggly front lawn. Sleazy graffiti covered the cream-colored walls of the clinic, some of which had been scrubbed away. Being near the end of the workday, most of the parking lot spaces were empty.

Paula pulled into a space closest to the entrance but didn't move her hands from the wheel.

"Here?" Lou asked. "This is where I'm supposed to find the replacement body? Or do you need me to pick out the cat you want to put me in?"

"Head vet fits what you describe. She's not exactly the buff babe of your dreams, but she does a lot of hiking from what I see on her Instagram."

"You use Instagram?" Lou shook her head. "Wait, so you want to take out the only veterinarian in town? The person you sold the practice to?"

Paula shrugged. "Why not? There are other people who work here, you know."

"Aren't people going to notice if she goes missing?"

"It's a Saturday, Lou. The clinic is closed on Sundays, and by Monday, you'll be in her body."

"But if it's me—I don't know how to be a vet, Paula."

"For the last time, it is *Grandma* Paula to you, and that ain't my problem, kiddo. Once it's your body, it's your life. You're going to have to figure it out." She tapped her finger against Lou's head wound, the nail nicking the soft flesh. "Use that big brain of yours, summa cum laude."

"People *need* her, Grandma. There's farmers out here that—"

"Again, not my problem. Besides, I don't like her much to begin with, and neither does anyone else. She's kind of a prude."

"Then why did you sell your practice to her?" Lou's ears broiled with anger. She was sure steam was seeping out of them like a tea kettle on a burner. "At a loss, for Chrissake!"

She stared at her. "You know about that?"

"Yes! Max told me."

"Hmm." Paula pushed back the cuticles on the fingernails of her right hand. "All I can say to that, sweetie, is when you get to be my age, you're going to understand the pressure behind 'Out with the old, in with the new.'" Her eyes seemed far away now, and her voice quieted. "Didn't matter that I'd given 30 years of service to this community. Your hands shake a little one time and suddenly the patients start driving to the next town over and calling up your son like you're on your deathbed."

Lou doubted that was why the patients had fled her grandmother's practice, but she didn't push it.

"When you're young, you get to make choices. Then other people make them for you."

She swallowed back the anger crawling up inside her, its fingers pricking the back of her throat. *No*, she wanted to say. When you're young, other people will *still* make choices for you. They will choose to hit you with a baseball for breaking a window. They will choose to send you to bed without supper when you don't want to eat the freezer-burnt broccoli that expired three months ago and made your mouth taste nauseatingly sour.

They will rip your best friend from her bed and force her outside on one of the coldest winter afternoons to go ice-fishing, even though she said she didn't feel good.

"Day's a wastin'." Paula moved to unclip her seat buckle, and Lou's stomach somersaulted. They were here. In town—albeit a very remote part of town—and she had options. Now was her time to turn on the charm.

"Does she know you don't like her?" Lou asked.

"What?"

"Also, isn't she going to immediately be suspicious? You don't have a pet. At least, not one you could bring to a vet. Why would you be here to begin with?"

Paula pressed her lips together. "I know what you're trying to do."

"I-I'm being serious! I—Look, do you have my phone? Pull out my phone. My roommate has a dog. I could tell her I was here to visit my grandma, my dog got injured, and he's in the back; I need help moving him in."

"And why do you need your phone?"

Shit. "B-because I can show her a picture of the dog—"

"If you're a good enough actor, you should be able to convince her you have an injured dog that's truly in need of help. You don't need your phone to do that. And in this scenario, *I* could also claim that I own a dog. *I* could be the person that goes in."

Lou glanced down at her restraints. Beaming, she held them up with pride. "N-no, you can't! Look! You'd have to untie me if you wanted me to be the getaway driver. And I know you don't want to risk leaving me alone with your truck. Then you'd lose. And again, small town! Who's seen you at the county shelter? Who's seen you with a dog? No one!"

Never in her life did she think she'd advocate for a kidnapper to *not* release her from custody and give her the keys to a truck. Then again, she wouldn't want the truck anyway. Paula could easily report it missing before she'd have a chance to save Max.

Fingernails tapped against the steering wheel. "What are you suggesting? That I untie you and send you in there by yourself?"

Lou gulped.

"Absolutely not." She yawned and ruffled her hair, unbothered. "If I let you go in there by yourself, there's no telling what you'll do."

"But we need a getaway car. We have to do this fast. I'm trying to cooperate with you, Pa—Grandma."

Paula stared at her. Then, "Two minutes. You don't come out in two, and I'm going to make an even bigger dent in that head of yours."

Lou considered this. Two minutes. Two minutes to come up with a plan. Couldn't call the cops. As a queer person who lived in Minneapolis, where the former chief of police was a notable white supremacist, she didn't like the idea of trying that in this small ass town. With the ridiculousness of her story and how disheveled she looked—big ass head wound, scratches and blood all over her face—who would believe her? She'd be mistaken for a junkie and laughed off before she could save her skin.

That meant she would have to take the two minutes to go inside, wait it out, and bait Paula to enter. If she and the veterinarian got the upper hand, Lou could get the truck, rescue Max, and get the hell out of here.

Her only shot.

Paula reached for her switchblade and used it to cut Lou's restraints. While she rubbed her swollen wrists her grandmother drove the truck around the backside of the building. It was a tight squeeze, just as Lou remembered, given the massive dumpster and biological waste containers crowding the area. No one ever parked back here except the patients who had to put their pets down. Paula would let them leave out the back door so no one had to see them cry. It was the only time Lou ever remembered her grandmother being kind toward a human being. Maybe that was what Max had seen in her. Superficial acts of kindness that obscured the dark person hidden beneath. Like the Titanic iceberg, nothing seemed quite that horrible—or deadly—until you dove below the murky waters.

"What's the dog's name?" Paula asked.

"Does it matter?"

"Of course it does."

"Uh . . . Brownie?"

Paula paused to consider this. She squinted at Lou. "You're a writer, aren't you?"

"Kinda."

"Then you should know that's a stupid fucking name." She shook her head. "Lordy, I sure hope my new children don't turn out as braindead as you."

Lou bristled with anger and moved to exit, but as soon as she did, Paula snatched her back. She preened and groomed her, rearranging her flyaway hairs. When that was finished, she licked her thumb and used it to wash away some of the dirt and blood on her face.

"Kitty wash," Paula explained, unsmiling. "Now go get our girl."

TEN

ONE OF THE PERKS OF living in a small town was that people didn't lock their doors, and garages were left wide open. The vet's clinic was no exception. Lou slipped in with ease, greeted by a cacophony of dogs barking and a single parakeet ready to raise hell. None of them were visible, but in her distant memory, she recalled the cages were closer to the west side of the building. A small hallway extended in front of her that led to some examination rooms, offices, and the receptionist's area in the front.

The veterinarian stuck her head out of the doorway of her office, fork in hand, chewing ravenously as though she had not eaten all day. She probably hadn't. For a moment, Lou felt bad for her, but then she remembered how little time she had. She took in the woman's face, soft and round, her jawline undefined. Her hair was more of a strawberry blond, with eyelashes to match. She looked like someone you'd find on a cottagecore Pinterest board or in an art history textbook. She wasn't drop dead gorgeous by any means, but shit. For a moment, Lou contemplated what life would be like in her body, but shame slapped the idea out of her head.

The vet frowned. "Can I help you?"

"I-I need you to listen to me carefully."

Suddenly Lou felt woozy. Shit, shit, shit. Was she dehydrated, nervous, or dealing with residual effects from that random drug she'd used? But that had worn off earlier. Wait—no. Paula had said the effects lasted longer than she thought they would. Lou thought she had just been saying that to get her to not tell Max about what happened to Kelsea. That meant this was a cyclical thing. Her metabolism hadn't burnt through the drug.

The muscles in her calves spasmed, causing her to lean against the wall and slide down it, her hope sinking with her. Beads of sweat gathered along her hairline and rolled down her blood-freckled cheeks. Her heartbeat echoed in her ears like the drumming of an ancient song and time became molasses.

The veterinarian muttered curse words underneath her breath and retreated into the office before returning to hover over her, now with a mask covering the lower half of her face. "Not another ivermectin user. Get fucking vaccinated."

"W-what?" Lou whispered, black spots dancing in front of her eyes. "I—I don't—"

"You don't believe in them, yeah, yeah, yeah. Not my problem, loser. Get the hell out of here or I'm calling the cops."

"I'm vaxxed. I need . . . huh-h-he-help." She had to squeeze the words from her chest in order to say them. "Hunted."

"Hunted?" The veterinarian crouched down beside her, brow furrowed. Now that she was up close, Lou could make out what was engraved on her name tag. Rosalyn. Beautiful name for a beautiful woman. "It's not hunting season."

Lou felt the seconds ticking away. Panic ballooned within her chest, fixing to burst. With what feeble strength she had, she grabbed Rosalyn's hand, shaking it over and over again.

"Weapon," she whispered.

Confused, Rosalyn didn't leave. Her delicate fingers reached up to touch the wound on Lou's head. "When did you get this wound? It's deep. You might have a concussion."

Lou jerked away from her and hit her head against the cement wall. Pain exploded in her head as though she had been attacked with a thousand stones. Rosalyn huffed in frustration, placing her hands on her waist.

"*Weapon*!" Lou reiterated, all facets of language failing her.

Rosalyn shrank away from her, eyes wide and wary. *No.* Lou recognized what that look meant. Threat. The vet thought she was threatening her. It was almost comical, how horribly this was going. Tears watered in Lou's eyes at the hilarity of it all. Her head spun in circles like a Tilt-a-Whirl as her stomach gurgled in response to the quiet comprehension Paula would soon shoulder-check her way through that door and assault—possibly *kill*—yet another person right in front of her.

Trembling, Lou lifted her arm and pointed toward the back door. "Her."

Rosalyn's head turned in the direction of the door. From the way her expression shifted, it seemed like she finally understood there was a threat lying on the other side of it. She leapt to her feet, shoulders squared, and rushed back into her office, presumably to grab a weapon. Lou's eyelids flickered like the lightbulb in an attic of a dusty house. She was unable to focus, the dance of the black spots growing more and more aggressive.

The back door creaked open, and Lou's heart rammed into her ribcage like a car wreck. Rosalyn stumbled out of her office, phone in one hand and a pink canister of pepper spray in the other. Paula shuffled inside. She looked at Lou with disappointment, nostrils flaring, eyes reproachful. Rosalyn shuffled nervously in place, unsure of what to do. To Lou's dismay, she lowered her hands. Paula immediately noticed the canister, and began to rifle around in her purse.

"Paula," Rosalyn said. "What are you doing here?"

Paula continued to dig in her purse. "I am *so* sorry about my granddaughter. She's a little woozy from the heat."

"That's—why are you here?"

Paula laughed, and her hand slowly slid out from the bag. Lou's heartbeat drummed in her ears, thinking she was about to unsheathe her knife, but she saw Paula only pulled out a packet of wet wipes. Paula waddled over to Lou and crouched down, then began to swipe away the sweat on her face.

"Oh Lou," Paula fussed. "Look at what you've done. I told you to drink more water."

"I was getting ready to close up shop for the night, so . . ."

"She's in town visiting for the wedding." Lou's head slowly turned away from Paula, the muscles in her neck becoming soup, and Paula gripped her chin and jerked her upright. "You know."

Rosalyn's mouth set in a grim line. "Oh. Right. You and Max."

"Oh, you know about it?"

"I don't think there are many people in town who *don't* know about it." She scratched the back of her head. Lou's eyes almost watered when she saw the veterinarian slip the pepper spray into the pocket of her lab coat. "So this is your granddaughter?"

"Yes! Um, she's re—I mean, disabled. Disabled. Autism. Nonverbal. Other cognitive disorders."

"She . . ." Rosalyn's eyes narrowed. "She doesn't seem nonverbal. She came in here talking about a weapon."

"Oh, you know, she's *very* big on that little *She-Ra* show right now. The one with the sword or whatever?"

"I know the one. Can't say I care much for cartoons though. But that doesn't really answer my question, Paula."

"What?"

"Why are you here?"

"*Oh.* Because—well—I wanted to show her around town. She grew up here. Used to come to the veterinary office with me. And I thought we'd pop in through the back like old times. But the darn girl!" Paula squeezed Lou's cheeks like a stress toy. "Took off without me! What can you do?"

"Did you drive here?"

"Yes! Truck's parked out back."

"So she's disabled, but she can undo a seatbelt?"

Lou's eyes widened. Her body wouldn't cooperate, but she was hoping her facial expressions would get Rosalyn's attention. *Yes! You're right! She's full of shit! Get the pepper spray out!* Rosalyn squinted and her jaw set in a firm line.

"Why is she all—she's got a wound on her head."

Paula's voice grew taut with impatience. "Some autistic people hit themselves. You don't know that?"

"Forgive me for being concerned when someone comes stumbling in through my back door mumbling something about a weapon. And in the future, if you want to visit, I'd prefer for you to come in through the front door, not the back. That's exactly what I told you last time you visited, remember? When those cats went missing?"

Missing cats? Lou's stomach churned. That couldn't have been for any good reason. Maybe she had been seeking additional bodies for her experiments. Beloved family pets or sickly strays, she'd scoop into carriers and whisk them away in the middle of the afternoon, never to be seen again.

"I know, I know, but we didn't want to trouble you! Or the receptionist . . ." Paula's eyes fixed on Rosalyn, waiting for her to confirm whether or not she was alone. The receptionist's desk was not visible from the hallway.

"She's already left for the day. And again, come in through the front door, please." Rosalyn shoved her hands in the pockets of her lab coat. "Preferably not at the end of the day. I gotta close up shop."

"Of course, of course. We are *so* sorry to interrupt your busy schedule. We'd best be on our way."

"Yep."

"Can you—can you help me get her into the car? My back isn't as strong as it used to be, and my doctor said my hip'd give out if I lift things that are too heavy." Paula's voice lowered to a scandalous whisper. "Or worse, my pelvic floor. And I'm sure you just finished mopping, so I wouldn't want to make closing up shop any harder for you."

Rosalyn smiled thinly in response. "Sure. I'll help."

She rolled her eyes and crouched down beside Lou, who whined wordlessly in protest. Paula swooped her arm underneath Lou's armpit, and together they heaved her to her feet, then hobbled out the door. Lou's heartbeat pulsated throughout her body. *No, no, no.* The blistering bright light of the dying sun flooded her eyes, and she squinted in pain. With her free hand, Paula fished in her purse for her keys and unlocked the truck. They set Lou on the passenger seat. Paula leaned in to buckle her up and glared ferociously at her.

"Thank you so much, Ros." Paula cracked open the dashboard and withdrew a round spool of twine, which she began to wrap around Lou's wrists. She was being kidnapped again, in broad daylight. *For fuck's sake.*

Rosalyn, concerned citizen that she was, didn't move. "Are you supposed to do that?"

"How else am I supposed to stop her from hitting herself, silly?"

"You're not supposed to restrain autistic people."

Paula snapped off the end of the twine and finished her knot. Her smile stretched from ear to ear, her pupils pinpricks, the whites bloodshot. She closed the door and slowly turned back to face Rosalyn. Lou groaned, pressing her head against the window.

"You should untie her, Paula. That material is rough on her skin."

"Oh? And you think you're a fucking expert?"

Oh shit. Paula's mask had dropped. The little, seemingly frail woman was now squared off against Rosalyn, who stared back at her in disgust. She shook her head and reached into her pocket for her phone.

"Actually, yes. I have an autistic cousin."

Paula tittered as though she found that amusing. "Look, dear. I don't mean to be cross with you, but I'm her grandmother. Trust that I know how to take care of her."

Rosalyn shook her head. Her other hand stretched into the pocket of her lab coat.

"What do you think you're doing?"

"Something's not right here." Rosalyn shrugged her shoulders as she continued to touch the screen of her phone. "Maybe if I hadn't caught you trespassing again, I would let this slide, but—"

"Then why don't you lock your stupid door, bitch?" Paula's voice had lowered to a snarl, and although Lou couldn't clearly see her face, she knew her lips were drawn back, teeth bared, ready to bite. "Huh? You got a fancy little smartphone like that, but you've never heard of a lock?"

"Um, because the fucking lock is broken, like almost everything else in that ratchet building you sold me. You know how I have to lock that door at night? I have to push a big ass filing cabinet in front of it."

"It's not my fault you won't fix your door. That's the problem with your generation. You whine and whine and complain about the things everyone before you broke, but you'll invest none of the effort in getting it fixed."

"You know what? You're right. I'm not only going to fix that door, but I'll get a whole entire security system. Cameras. Lights. Fucking laser beams. Anything to keep your entitled old ass from wandering onto my property again, and stealing shit for your junkie boyfriend—"

"How dare you! He is *not* a junkie!"

"Then why did all those chemicals disappear?"

"My boyfriend is *not* a junkie, and I didn't steal anything from you!" Paula jabbed a furious finger into her chest, and Rosalyn's jaw dropped, appalled. Suddenly, Paula deflated, her shoulders melting into her form, making her appear smaller. "Wait a minute. Did you say you don't have cameras out here?"

Rosalyn flinched. "I mean—"

"That makes this so much easier."

Paula reached into her purse, whipped out her switchblade, and smacked the handle square into Rosalyn's nose. The bone shattered and the entire structure shifted sharply to the right. Geysers of blood erupted from both nostrils, spraying the front of her shirt and lab coat. Rosalyn lifted her free hand to shield her face, and the other continued to fumble with her phone. Lou braced herself. *She's angry enough to finish this right here.* She expected her grandmother to flick open the knife and slash her straight across the face—

—but instead she tackled her to the ground. It was almost comical, how the small woman had leapt upon her and how the other tumbled like a skyscraper on a demolition site. Bone crunched against concrete and an anguished, short shout escaped Rosalyn's mouth. The contents of Paula's purse spilled everywhere, and the phone that had been in Rosalyn's hand spun away, mere inches out of reach. Paula straddled her body, the veins in her bony little hands visibly flexing as she raised the knife over her head. With a hideous cackle, Paula drove the handle into Rosalyn's skull and the woman's head snapped backward, cracking against the pavement. Her eyelids fluttered shut and her jaw went slack.

For a moment, it was silent. Paula's shoulders heaved as she tried to catch her breath.

Then slowly, a noise rose in the background. It started with a few meager meows and barks, accumulating more, until gradually a chorus of dogs and cats echoed from the shelter. Their sound was discordant and nonsensical; rhythmless, but not lacking power or emotion. It reminded Lou of the death songs the crows sung when circling the frozen lakes in the winters, ravenous and hateful, baiting passerby to fall through the ice so they could peck the eyes from their drowned bodies.

Bewildered, but unperturbed, Paula dragged Rosalyn's body by her feet over to her truck. Every time her skull bumped against a crack in the pavement, the animals' song grew louder and louder. Although the audio was muffled through the windows of the truck, Lou could swear she heard the steel bars on their cages rattling in protest, as if they were demanding to be let out.

The animals knew exactly how this would end.

ELEVEN

"GODDAMN IT." PAULA SLAPPED LOU across her face, but she didn't feel the sting. "What the hell's wrong with you?"

Lou didn't know, but she had a sinking feeling her body had decided to give up on itself. She must have passed out. Maybe with the fear of death on the line, it decided to shut down. Turn off the brain, turn off the muscles, turn off the lights. Her limbs were paralyzed, and the only sensation that coursed through her body was her own heartbeat and some slight tingling in her fingers. She couldn't wiggle her toes or move her legs. She wanted to giggle at the thought. Whatever bizarre drug Paula had concocted and injected into her veins was now backfiring on her.

"No!" Paula whined. She rummaged around in her purse. "You *have* to sober up. You got to! How else am I going to get this bitch in my truck?"

Outside the truck, Rosalyn lay on the ground, mouth still open, her face turned into the dirt. A fly landed on the inside of her lip and crept across the fleshy surface.

"I do *so* much for you," Paula said, emotion thickening her voice.

"I invite you here, I get you the body you want, and you can't even help me put it in the truck. I need *one* thing to go right in my life—oh, sweet Lord, there it is."

Uh-oh. Another syringe, another opportunity for Lou to be filled with chemicals that would fry her system. Strangled sounds escaped her mouth, but Paula rolled her eyes, removed the cap, and popped it into her vein. Every single synapse ignited like fireworks. Lou inhaled sharply, sucking air into her lungs, re-inflating them. The black spots evaporated, but her vision still seemed a little fuzzy and out of focus at the edges, as if viewing the world through a fisheye lens.

Paula smiled at her. "You feel better?"

Lou nodded.

"Good." Paula glanced down at Lou's restraints and rolled her eyes. She slammed her fist against the dashboard and wailed in frustration, spittle flying from her mouth. "Goddamn it!" She slipped the knife through and cut them off. "God—fucking—*damn it!*"

Lou winced, squeezing her eyes shut. This whole nightmarish trip was nothing if not a reminder of what it had been like to grow up with this banshee. Always upset with someone, never at fault for anything. Her parents had done their best to defend her from Paula's tantrums, but their work schedules were not nearly as stable and consistent as hers was. Every Saturday and Sunday, the house became a football game, and Lou had to play defense. Sometimes she won and could escape, unnoticed, to the yard with Max and Kelsea. Other times she would be belted and screamed at until white noise filled her skull, rendering her numb. During these times, her only solace was crawling into her closet and pulling her clothes on top of her, forming an insulated little pile that kept her cozy and dried her tears.

She would give anything to crawl inside a clothing pile now. Instead she was being forced from the truck and told to lift a beautiful woman she didn't know into the bed of the vehicle. Feeling had not completely restored in her arms, and her muscles shook with exertion as she threw Rosalyn over the side. She heard another sickening crack and winced.

"Do you want another body or not?" Paula hissed, snapping her fingers in her face. "Then you had better be fucking gentle, because if I have to reset more bones, we're going to have a problem."

"No ma'am." Lou's ears buzzed as she spoke. The noise rattled through her ear canals, tingling the skin and microscopic hairs filling the space. Images of a fly akin to the one that crawled on Rosalyn's lips flashed through her mind, its hairy wilted body twisting through the earwax-clogged space. She smacked the heel of her palm against her head.

"What are you doing that for?" Paula snapped.

"Something's wrong." Her voice split into two different registers, one high, and one low.

Paula shrugged her shoulders. "I don't know what to tell you, girlie. You're going to have to ride it out."

"What did you inject me with?"

"What did I inject you with—nothing stronger than the weed I used to smoke back in the day. I thought you were a hardcore stoner."

While it was true that Lou used CBD oils and gummies to manage her anxiety, they lacked THC. Lou felt as though her brain was molting. She could see globs of its waxy, fatty membrane sloughing off its surface and dripping into the cavern of her skull. "Grandma, I need to sit down."

"Oh, *fine!*" she snarled, shaking her head.

Lou stumbled back to the truck, her limbs still functional but her brain completely fucked. Paula didn't climb in the driver's seat. She moved to the truck bed and pulled a cerulean tarp over Rosalyn's body. "We don't have time for this, Louella! It's only a matter of time before Maxie wakes up, and he's out there *suffering* in this blasted heat!"

I didn't want to leave him in the van, Lou thought, gnawing on the inside of her cheek. Strips of flesh peeled away with a gentle swipe of her tongue. She stuck out her tongue. She wiped her tongue with her fingers, trying to remove the grimy bits that filled her mouth. Nothing came out except wet streaks of saliva.

Paula climbed into the driver's seat and scowled when she saw Lou's wet hands. "You're drooling?"

Lou swiped at the liquid bubbling from her mouth. It was frothy, like the bubbles in an ice-cold glass of milk. She could imagine its creamy, sweet yet neutral taste. Suddenly she wanted to suck on her fingers.

"Don't do that!" Paula smacked Lou's hand away from her face. "You're not a baby."

"You shouldn't have drugged me."

"You shouldn't have made my life so difficult. You ever think about that?" Paula gritted her teeth. She turned the keys in the ignition. She began to back out of the narrow space.

"You're going to leave the animals there?"

"Don't be a fucking moron, for Chrissakes. Someone will be there to check on them in the morning. Again, it's not like this bitch is the only one who works there. Fuck, how many times do I have to tell you something before you listen?"

The truck engine roared as Paula hit the gas, and she nearly hit the curb as she hightailed it out of the parking lot. Lou twisted to look over her shoulder, trying to see if Rosalyn had moved. A bit of the tarp had slipped off her body, but it hadn't exposed her completely.

"Did you remember to tie her up?"

Paula revved the engine as she sped through a yellow light. Her knuckles whitened as she tightened her grip on the steering wheel. Lou kept her eyes on Rosalyn's body rolling around in the back of the truck.

"You might want to slow down—"

"Shut up." Paula glowered at her. "You've ruined everything, you know that? You and your father."

Lou could no longer make sense of any of Paula's diatribes. In her intoxicated state she was having a hard time separating fact from fiction. It wasn't her fault; it was her fault. Her body was her father's and her grandmother's, an ecosystem of generational trauma spanning back further than she could comprehend. She stared at her grandmother.

Paula started to sob and fumbled in her purse for tissues but discovered she had none. Paula spewed cuss words and threw the bag at Lou, who barely flinched in response. A car honked as she turned without yielding.

For a moment, hope swelled within Lou's chest. Was her grandmother about to be undone by her own reckoning?

"What the fuck are you smiling about?" Paula asked.

"Nothing."

"You're a monster. Do you know that? You've always been a horrid little monster. Everything was about you, all the time. Why can't it be about me? Why can't it be about Max?"

The buildings disappeared from view as they drove out of town. Rosalyn's body continued to roll around in the truck bed, thudding every so often. It sounded like a drumbeat, and Lou couldn't help but tap her foot along to it. Every time she did, the noise reverberated through her body like she was a bell. Ahh, a body like a bell. To be a church bell ringing on the hour, every hour. To curve into yourself and outwards, never beginning but never quite ending—

"Do you not care about the people you've hurt, Lou? You *hurt* people. You hurt Max when you left here. And he still—that stupid, sweet boy—stuck his fucking neck out for you. He stood up for you so you could have the body *you* wanted, even when he was pissin' me off. Are you grateful?"

"Grateful. Cheese grater. Gratar—grator. Gator." Lou giggled to herself. Words? What were they?

"You owe him a lot. You owed him after what happened to Kelsea."

At the mention of her name, the buzz Lou had been enjoying evaporated. Gone were the all-body good vibes, and now she was firmly grounded in reality. Paula focused on the road ahead of them and shook her head with disappointment.

"You let that little girl drown in the lake that day. I know your parents told me not to tell you that, but you did."

An image of Kelsea surfaced in her mind. Ashen skin. Ashen like the flecks that fell down from the wintry sky the day they buried her. Lips open and waiting for flies like Rosalyn's. A blanket of lilies covering her in a bed of cherry oak. Glossy brown eyes forever closed. Lou remembered how cold her hand had felt even in the sweltering church.

Lou shook her head. "Not true."

"Listen to you. *Not true*. Of course it's true."

"No. She didn't want to go out on the ice that day, and her parents—"

"You both fell through the ice. And because of that, you forced Max to make a decision. You know who he saved? *You*. You, you selfish piece of shit. No one thought he should've saved you over his own sister. His parents won't even come to our wedding, and you had the *gall* to tell him he couldn't be happy. Shame on you. *Shame*."

The words seeped into Lou and infected her bloodstream. She shivered. She brought her legs up onto the seat and wrapped her arms around herself. She longed for the safety of her closet. For the warmth of Max's smiling face. For her to be anywhere but here. Shallow breaths rocked her chest as the tears rose. She *knew* the truth about what happened when she was young. She did not need Paula to so cruelly twist the knife into her; she had already done that herself.

Lou saw a blue lump emerge in the rearview mirror. Rosalyn. Rosalyn sat up in the truck bed. As soon as Lou opened her mouth to warn her grandmother a cop car came into view.

When the cop motioned for them to pull over, she realized he was parked right beside the mess of human remains Paula had told her not to worry about.

TWELVE

PAULA SLAMMED ON THE BRAKES and the truck came to a stop beside the police officer. The abrupt stop caused Rosalyn to smash into the back window. She moaned a little bit, although the cop didn't seem to hear her. The bald cop, head shining in the heat of the fading sun, walked over to the window and motioned for her to roll it down. Paula obliged and offered him her biggest smile.

"Good evening, Officer Massey." Her voice croaked a little as she spoke, as if to make her seem more fragile than she actually was. "How are you?"

"Mighty good, Paula. How're those wedding plans comin' along?"

"Good, good. Gonna happen this Monday," she said, flashing him her engagement ring.

He smiled but seemed perturbed by the idea. He wiped the sweat from his head and gestured to the destroyed crop field behind him. "You and your boy here—"

"Boyfriend. He's my boyfriend."

"Right. You live a little ways down this road, right?"

"Yes, yes . . . ohh . . ." Paula clicked her tongue against her teeth and shook her head at the destruction, as though she was seeing it for the first time. "You know, we get a lot of drunk kids on these backroads late at night."

"Zeke wanted me to come over here and check it out regardless. There appears to be a piece of roadkill here. Probably a deer. Big tire tracks in the mud, too."

"Aww, shoot. What a bummer."

"You haven't seen anything?"

"No, sir." Paula shook her head. "Like I said, probably the kids."

"Zeke said this wasn't here this morning."

"Officer Massey, I've been out running errands all day. I've got my granddaughter in town with me for the wedding and I haven't seen anything."

THUNK. One of Rosalyn's limbs smacked against the truck bed. Officer Massey frowned, glancing toward the back. Paula giggled, twisting a strand of hair around her finger.

"You got something there, Paula?"

Lou's heart sang in her chest. At this point, she'd take the help of a cop. Maybe if she let him on to what was happening, he wouldn't arrest her for kidnapping and attempted murder. Then again, even prison was better than being stuck in a truck with Paula. Lou made eye contact with the cop and her pupils shifted backward, gesturing to the truck bed. The cop noticed this and stared hard at Paula in turn, waiting for her answer.

"Stuff for the wedding." She smiled so hard she squinted. "Extra chairs for the reception. We're hosting at our place afterward. And some signs. Floral arrangements. You know how it is. We're going to have ourselves a barbecue and a bunch of booze. It'll be a mighty fun party. You oughta stop by."

"That sounds nice—" Another *thunk* interrupted his train of thought. A perplexed expression crossed his face. "You know, you should keep things strapped down in the truck bed to make sure things don't fly out."

Paula's fingertips drummed against the steering wheel, and Lou's stomach dropped. *Oh shit.* She jerked her head a little bit, encouraging the cop to check the back. The cop's hand moved to his holster.

"I'm going to need you to step out of the vehicle, ma'am."

Paula's jaw dropped. "What?"

"Just step on out of the vehicle."

The cop stared at Lou as Paula climbed out of the driver's seat, arms crossed, brow furrowed. Lou kept her hands folded across her lap and bounced her foot against the floor, trying to quiet her anxious nerves. Paula placed her hands on her hips, appraising the officer.

"What's this all about now?" Paula asked. She shot Lou a dirty look.

The cop didn't ask her to put her hands on her head. Maybe it was because he didn't think of her as a threat. But when he approached the truck Lou wanted to scream. And when Paula pulled the switchblade from the sleeve of her muumuu, Lou did scream.

The cop reached for his holstered gun but Paula mounted his back like a rodeo clown on a bull, wrapping her legs around his waist so he couldn't buck her off. Her manicured hand gripped his head like a melon, ready to be squashed. With one fluid motion, she sliced the knife across his carotid artery. Blood spurted over the tarp and cascaded down from the wound in his neck. Paula jumped off him and watched as he staggered backward, his eyes swelling with shock. He collapsed to the ground, convulsing.

Lou shrieked. "Why didn't you just hit him with the car?!"

"Please. Like we have time for that." Paula's eyes widened, and she shrieked, "Grab her!"

Lou turned to see Rosalyn rising from the truck bed, the blue tarp still wrapped around her body. Two bloodshot eyes stared at her. Rosalyn lifted a creaky knee onto the wheel well hump, then threw herself over the side of the truck bed, onto the asphalt. Lou rushed around to help her to her feet, but Rosalyn elbowed her away. The woman staggered to her feet, panting, wild strands of blond hair drifted in front of her face. Sunlight flickered off the back of her head, evoking a halo, yet her foul expression was anything but angelic.

"Don't you *dare* fucking touch me," she hissed, blood frothing in her mouth. She spat a wad of red phlegm onto the ground. "You are going to . . ." Her eyes spotted the slain officer and she released a ghostly shriek.

Paula rolled her eyes. "Nice fucking going, Lou. Wonder if ol' Zeke heard that one?"

Rosalyn turned and sprinted into the cornfields. Paula screamed at Lou, demanding she follow Rosalyn. But Lou shook her head ferociously. Paula slinked toward her, knife in hand, her expression menacing. Suddenly Lou was back in the yard of her childhood home, frozen in place, cowering as her grandmother came to deliver the licking of a lifetime.

"What the fuck are you doing?" Paula snarled.

"We have to stop this, Grandma. We have to—"

"You stupid fucking moron, you think she knows the difference between you and me? She thinks *you* helped me take her down! If you think you're going to get out of this . . ." Paula cupped her face in her hands, the knife nicking her cheek. The blood from the wound rolled down her face. "You're not! You're just not!"

Lou's eyes watered. "But I don't—"

"It's your fault I didn't think to tie her up to begin with!" Spit flew from Paula's mouth. "*Go after her!* That's *your* body, and I'm not getting you another one!"

Lou sprinted into the cornfield.

THIRTEEN

WHEN THEY WERE SEVEN, MAX, Kelsea, and Lou wandered into a cornfield together after they had spied a scarecrow holding what appeared to be a giant lollipop. Unbeknownst to them, the lollipop wasn't real, just an extra decoration for Halloween the farmer had decided to tack on. It didn't take five minutes before they were separated from each other and got lost within the maze. Terrified, Kelsea had cried these loud, gulping sobs that echoed through the rows like a homing beacon. Her cries reunited the three, and the sound of the road noise from truckers driving by led them out to the highway. On that day, Lou learned the key to getting through a cornfield was by listening closely to everything around you.

Unfortunately, Rosalyn didn't have that skill.

Winded and woozy, she was breathing so hard Lou heard her from several feet away. Lou weaved through the rows of stalks until, finally, she stood a few inches from her. Rosalyn screeched and darted to the left, scrambling away as fast as her wounded legs would carry her. Lou took a deep breath and charged after her and, once she had caught up, snatched her wrist. The woman screamed and twisted around, her free hand curved like a claw. She swiped it across Lou's face, knocking her backward.

Once again, Rosalyn began to run away from her, but this time when Lou caught her, she grabbed both of her wrists. She murmured soothing words to try to calm her down. Part of her still held out hope they could take down Paula if they worked together, but with the way this woman was fighting her, she was starting to worry about her own safety. The caterwauling reached a boiling point, and Lou's fingers dug into her soft flesh, threatening to break the skin. Rosalyn yelped in response.

"Listen to me!" Lou hissed through clenched teeth. "I'm trying to—"

"Fuck you, *freak!*"

Rosalyn spat blood onto Lou's face. Lou flinched and her hands moved up to wipe the gooey mess away, leaving herself exposed. Rosalyn tackled her, and several stalks of corn crunched beneath their bodies as they hit the ground. The air reeked of manure and pesticides as they rolled around on the ground, scratching and slapping at each other. Blood sprouted from the tiny wounds they nicked into each other's skin. Rosalyn managed to roll Lou onto her back and straddled her. Her fist connected with Lou's nose, and the pain shot into the back of her brain. *Shit, shit, shit.* She was losing fast, but she realized Rosalyn was still wearing her lab coat, now stained brown from their tussle. If Paula had forgotten to tie her wrists, had she forgotten Rosalyn was armed?

Lou wasted no time. She sprung forward, her hand slipping into the pocket of Rosalyn's lab coat. Lou removed the canister. Rosalyn shrieked, but it was too late. Lou snapped off the safety and pulled the trigger. A white mist shot through the air, spray painting Rosalyn's face and open eyes. Lou had attended many concerts in her life, but never had she come as close to bursting her own eardrums as when she heard that woman's shriek of pain.

Spiderwebs of angry red veins crisscrossed her pink sclera as redness flooded her body like an invasion of fire ants. Some of the mist particles recoiled onto Lou's skin, igniting it. Sobbing and spitting, Rosalyn rolled around on the ground, her body a closed fist. Desperate, Lou tried to wipe the mist away from her arms and legs, but all that did was spread the fiery hot pain over more of her body.

"Louella!" Paula screeched from the roadway. "Get over here, Louella!"

Lou staggered to her feet, hovering over the crumpled woman. She grabbed her and wrenched her upwards. Rosalyn's eyes were squeezed shut and she continued to howl in agony. Mucus obscured her nostrils and gobs of spit dribbled down her chin.

"Why are you doing this to me?" Rosalyn sobbed, her breaths escaping in hisses. "I didn't do anything to you!"

Lou winced. "I'm sorry."

Lou crouched down and picked up the pepper spray canister, then pocketed it. Despite the pain ravaging her body, for the first time today, she was thinking clearly.

"Please," she whispered through her tears. "The animals need me. They need me."

"I know," Lou said. "I'm trying to get us out of this. You have to cooperate."

"Fuck you!"

Yeah, there was nothing Lou could say to convince this woman she was on her side. It didn't matter. She had her plan, however basic it was. *Get back to the house. Rescue Max and Rosalyn. Spray Paula. Get the hell outta dodge.* She kicked the back of Rosalyn's ankle, forcing her forward. They weaved back through the corn stalks, toward the road, her captive blubbering the whole way. When Lou glanced up, she saw billows of smoke drifting through the air.

Fuck. Me.

As they emerged from the corn maze, Lou saw her grandmother standing by the cop car, a matchbook dangling between two fingers. Flames licked underneath the hood of the cop car, and smoke pooled out from it, drifting higher into the sky.

"What have you done?!" Lou screamed.

Paula stared back at her as though she was stupid. "Can't leave any evidence."

"You're going to burn down the entire fucking field, you psychotic bitch!" Rage sent her body into convulsions, but somehow she stood erect, shoulders squared. "You'll lead even *more* cops right to us! And you *just* killed one!"

"Why are you getting so angry at me? This is *your* fault." Paula shrugged her shoulders. "This wouldn't have happened if you took the hiker's body. Far as I'm concerned, her blood—and the officer's—is on your hands."

Lou pushed Rosalyn toward the truck before haphazardly throwing her over the edge of the truck bed. The woman wailed as her body hit the metallic surface with a hard crunch. Enraged, Lou stomped over to her grandmother. The little woman puffed up her chest and lifted her chin, indignant.

"You spread your fucking legs to one shitty man decades ago and you think the rest of the world owes you something. Well guess what? The world owes *me* something, Paula. It owes me something for putting up with your vile, malignant ass. I can't fucking believe I came back to help you. I can't believe I thought *you* would be the victim when it's Max! When it's *me!* I feel like I'm nine again!"

This whole time, Lou had been hesitant to hurt her grandmother, despite the hell she had put them through. Family, even fucked up and violent family, was still family. But now, with her mind sound and her body able, there would be nothing to hold her back from spilling their shared blood all over this fucking road.

As Lou raised the pepper spray canister, Paula raised something else, aimed, and fired. It happened so fast Lou didn't register what was going on until the pain shot through her body, ricocheting through all her nerve endings and forcing her to her knees.

This bitch had stolen the cop's taser.

Lou spasmed, unable to scream, her jaw clenched so tight it might as well have been wired shut. She writhed on the ground for several moments, her mind a complete blank. Paula, vulture that she was, circled her as if to admire her handiwork, but her expression lacked amusement. In fact, it was completely blank, as though all her emotions had been turned off. She hovered there for several moments before finally exhaling.

"Now we have even *less* time than before," Paula grumbled beneath her breath. Her foot connected with Lou's head, sending her rolling down into the ditch. As Lou lost consciousness, she heard her grandmother huff, "This is going to *kill* my fucking back."

FOURTEEN

LOU AWOKE IN A FAMILIAR place, but that didn't fill her with any less dread. She expected to feel the coolness of the stainless-steel table, but instead touched something hard, like stone. Her eyelids fluttered and she attempted to raise her aching head and take in her surroundings. Her body was slumped over on a chair and her wrists and ankles were bound together. Her fingers had been scraping against the tiled wall behind her.

To her surprise, she saw the stainless-steel table was occupied by Rosalyn, who was completely passed out and resting on her side. Her mouth hung open and loud, phlegm-laden snores escaped her sleeping body. Her skin was red and glistening from the pepper spray. In the background, hidden in the shadows of one of the countless iron cages occupying this room, Lou caught glimpses of calico-colored fur, but heard no sounds, and saw no little paws dangling from between the bars.

Paula had invested in a back-up plan.

Waves of panic wracked Lou's body as she remembered the events preceding this. The cop with the slit throat. The destroyed cornfield. The car fire Paula had started, which would inevitably spread. It was a hot summer, and an unusually dry one at that. Lou swore she could almost smell the smoke from the fields, even down in the basement. By the time the fire department got their shit together the whole house would be engulfed in flames. How long had she been out? Had the cat been there this whole goddamn time?

"Lou?"

She spun her head around to find him. He sat right beside her, bound to his chair in the same way she was. His wilted eyes drooped downward like crescent moons, gray puddles of exhaustion pooled beneath them. He looked almost as old as the woman he loved.

"Hey." He didn't smile. "You feeling okay?"

"What kind of dumb fucking question is that?"

He hesitated. Then, "You're right."

"I feel like shit. That's how I fucking feel." Lou tugged at her restraints, grinding her teeth. "And if we don't find a way to get out of here, we're fucked. You included."

"Me? Why?"

"She killed a cop and lit the cornfield on fire to try to get rid of his car."

"What the hell?!"

"Are you honestly surprised at *any* awful thing she does at this point?" Lou's heartbeat caught in her throat, and her eyes welled with tears, but she managed to keep it together. "We have to get out of here before the fire reaches the house."

"What are we supposed to do?"

"I don't know. I don't fucking know."

The rolling cart had been moved closer to the table, and the toolbox was open. An arsenal of sterile tools lay on a turquoise exam drape. One of them was an electric razor, which rested next to a car battery with a comically oversized off-switch affixed to its top. Two thin wires that looked like ethernet cables were clamped to the battery's terminals.

"How does she do this? Have you watched her do it?"

He didn't reply.

"Max?"

"I have. Yeah. She—she cracks open the skull and then hooks it up with a bunch of wires, and then to the car battery. Jumps it. Causes the brains to get scrambled and transfer the consciousness over."

"She connects people's brains to *car batteries*?"

"Yes." He wet his lips, his voice hoarse. "She's going to prepare this lady's brain to receive your signal, then when your brain gets zapped, you'll transfer over and take control."

"This is insane. This is so fucking insane."

"She made all those creatures you saw before. If Paula can make something like that, why can't you believe she'll pull this off?"

"Are you fucking kidding me? This isn't about her 'pulling this off,' Max. She killed two people in front of us today, and kidnapped another. And you're the one who encouraged her to kickstart *all* of this."

He gnawed on the inside of his cheek. "I think I can talk her down."

"Yeah, you fucking think," Lou spat, anger building in her body. "I mean, Jesus, you wanted to get your rocks off with an old lady, you could've picked *anyone* else. You have every nursing home in Crow Wing County to choose from, and they probably aren't psychotic, narcissistic mad scientists."

"I didn't *know* she was this bad."

"That's fucking debatable. Why? Why her?"

"You don't get it."

"*No.* Why her?"

Max bit his lip. He squeezed his eyes shut as though that could tune out the sound of Lou's voice.

"You deplorable piece of shit," she snarled. "She's going to kill us all. The least you could do is tell me what I'm dying for."

"Because she was all I had left."

"All you had left?"

"Yes." Silent tears rolled down his cheeks. "She—you—fuck, Lou. I don't know. Do you ever feel like you're perpetually in a state of losing things? And you—you'd give anything for it to end?"

"I don't understand."

"I lost Kelsea. I lost my parents. But I never thought I would lose you. And being with Paula—that was a way of holding onto what was important to me."

"You're telling me I was so important to you that you wanted to fuck my grandmother?"

"Kinda." He shrugged his shoulders, lowering his gaze. "I mean, if you want to put it that way, you can."

"Again, are you *sure* you're not in love with me? Kinda sounds like you're in love with me, dude."

"No, I'm not," he insisted, tension thick in his voice. "You're like a sister to me. You're like . . ."

He drifted off for a moment, quietly weeping. Tears irrigated the sweat and dirt caked onto his cheeks, washing it away. Lou remembered the last time she saw Max cry. They had been standing in the pews at the Lutheran church, their hands clasped together, the adults glaring at them with deep contempt. *How could Max have saved her over his own sister?* the bastards had whispered. Apparently the fuckers didn't know drowning was silent. Max had watched Lou fall through the ice in front of him, and he ran to help her. But Kelsea, whose throat had been hoarse from an awful cold that day, didn't make a scream when she plummeted through. By the time Max had tugged Lou back onto the surface of the ice, she was gone. They spent a lifetime telling themselves what happened wasn't their fault, carrying the weight of their failure on their backs while the adults shouldered no responsibility.

"You were gone. Kelsea's gone. My parents are gone. My own parents, Lou. My own parents didn't take me with them. And you know why? It's because—it's because of what happened to her." He gritted his teeth, eyes still closed. "Paula was the only one that wouldn't leave."

Kelsea was the one to drown in that lake, but Max and Lou were the ghosts left behind to navigate the hellish afterlife. Every birthday every Halloween, every Christmas that had passed since then was like peeling a scab off an old wound, a painful reminder someone was permanently missing at their cafeteria table, from all of their photographs, from every fucking March 18th. God, why? There was no God. Only a sadist would be so cruel as to rip a sweet little girl away from the world.

Lou could no longer ignore the real reason she had cut Max from her life. It was because he looked like Kelsea. Those cherry tomato cheeks, the way his eyes crinkled when he laughed, even his greasy hair was the exact shade of honey brown as hers. Every time she looked at him, she wasn't grateful he had saved her, no, she was horrified by the person she had ripped from this world. The survivor's guilt had poisoned her, and there was no antidote.

But maybe talking about it would help.

Lou swallowed a breath. A halfhearted smile tugged at the corner of her lips. "Really speaks to your character, the fact an actual psychopath would be the only one to stick it out with you."

"Fuck you." He chuckled for the briefest of moments, but then the grief resurfaced. "I know I didn't call you, but . . . to tell you the truth, I was worried about it."

"You were?"

"Hell yeah. You had that new life in the big city. I knew as soon as you told me you were going to meet other people who'd be more important to you. You always said you wanted to meet more queer people, and . . . well . . . I don't know. It's kinda like when an artist is in the middle of making his next painting. If you interrupted him when he was using his brush, you could risk ruining things. And then you became the guy that, y'know, wrecked the masterpiece."

Shame. Max thought she was ashamed of him and where they came from. Guilt sunk within her stomach and twisted in her intestines like a bird building its nest. Maybe shame had been a part of it, but it wasn't the entire explanation for why she left him behind.

"All these years . . . you didn't miss me at all, did you?"

"I didn't," Lou replied gently. "And I'm sorry I didn't. But I know it's not your fault. It wasn't because of who you are as a person. It was because . . ."

Everything. The house she'd grown up in. The lake where Kelsea had drowned. This nowhere-town stuck in time. All of it was a reminder not of the joys they were able to scrabble together in their ill-fated friendship, but of the struggles they were not meant to endure. Lickings and lashings from drunk parents to butter sandwich lunches to long nights spent alone, parented by a TV. Latchkey kids grew up with no one but each other, and when they lost one of their own—

—well, for Lou, that shattered her illusion that everything in her life was okay. When Kelsea drowned in that lake and the adults pointed fingers at her and Max, she thought of their neglect, of their obstinate refusal to accompany them, all the times they had dismissively waved their hands and told them to go play somewhere so they could slink away from their responsibilities. Kelsea didn't even want to get out of bed that day. She had a fever. Had her parents listened, they would still have their daughter, and her life would not have fallen into their young son's hands.

Lou thought about Paula's rants on ageism. The supposed "disrespect" she experienced wasn't ageism, but people refusing to cater to a narcissist's every whim. Even her father's pressure for her to sell the veterinary clinic wasn't ageism, but due to the fact she was an incompetent, dangerous individual. In truth, Lou decided, Paula was not old enough or incapacitated enough to truly experience the bouts of ageism, but it had only been ten years ago when Lou and Max were victims to it. Today, Lou understood no one—absolutely no one—was more disrespected in this world than a child.

"What are we . . ." His lips quivered, though he managed to stifle his sobs. "What are we going to do? How are we going to get out of here?"

Lou scanned the darkness for something of use. She spotted her bracelet, halfway across the room, its blade glinting in the faint light. It rested on top of the counter where she had found the beaker.

"My bracelet. If we could somehow get to it, we could use it to cut the ropes."

"I like that plan. Only one problem, Captain. How are we supposed to get over there?"

Lou pushed her feet against the ground. Her ankles were bound together, but she found if she used her whole body and wiggled it from side to side, she could scoot the chair forward a bit. Max laughed, eyes wide with surprise. It still didn't change the fact their wrists and ankles were bound, but if they scooted over there, they could probably figure out a way to pick up the bracelet. Maybe if someone was able to get it in their teeth, somehow, they could slice through someone's ropes.

Wriggling their bodies like worms, the two began to scooch across the floor. Lou's core muscles burned as she inched along. She couldn't help but laugh. In a sickening way, this reminded her of that time they went to the county fair and raced each other down the giant slide. They had to go down it on rucksacks that left carpet burns on their bums similar to the red welts encircling their wrists.

THUNK, THUNK, THUNK. They stopped dead in their tracks, listening to the heavy footsteps from upstairs.

They wouldn't be alone much longer.

FIFTEEN

MAX AND LOU REMAINED FROZEN to their spots as they listened to the door creak open and Paula shuffle down the stairs. The disheveled woman soon appeared in the doorway, her face glistening as though she had freshly washed it, her long hair bundled together and tied up in a surgical cap. Green scrubs covered her from head to toe, and the sight of her made Lou nauseous. *Ludicrous. Aren't you supposed to put surgical garb on in a sterile room, right before you go into surgery? She put that shit on in her musty-ass bedroom and came downstairs?* She waited with bated breath to see if her grandmother noticed they had moved, but no sense of recognition surfaced in her eyes. Or maybe she didn't care. Maybe she was arrogant enough to think she had won already.

"Sugarplum," Max beckoned to her. "You don't have to do this. You can let Lou go. We can work this out."

Lou shot Max a foul look, but he didn't even glance in her direction. Paula unhooked the mask looped around her mouth and smiled at them, but her eyes were unkind.

"We're not letting Lou go now. Not when we're this close." Her mouth turned downward, each end drooping to the end of her chin. "And you should know better than to suggest that to me at this point, muffin. You're the one that wanted to find a replacement body for her in the first place. If we had done what I wanted to do, we wouldn't be in this mess." She wagged her finger at him. "This is what you get for thinking you're smarter. I've been around the block longer than you have, kiddo. Never forget that."

"Don't call me kiddo." Max's voice hardened. "Paula, I'm not marrying you if you do this to Lou. It's time to give up. We can still build a life together. We can still—"

Cackles escaped Paula's wet lips, and she reared backward, slapping her knee. Hurt surfaced in Max's mournful brown eyes. Despite everything that happened, he still expected Paula to take his feelings into account. Still thought there was some sort of good in her that would make her reconsider her choices. God, Lou didn't know how this idiot so stubbornly tried to see the best in people. She couldn't tell whether it was a skill or a fatal flaw, but in this case, it seemed to be the latter.

"Aww, lover boy." Paula squeezed his cheeks together, then slapped one, but it was so light it didn't leave a mark. "Come hell or come high water, I was going to start this life over in another body. I wanted you to be a part of that more than anything, but it's clear to me now you can't be. You know why?"

Max swallowed. "Why?"

"You're too young for me."

"Told you," Lou muttered to him.

"And you've got this youthful optimism I used to think was . . . well, I used to think it was sweet, but now I find it so goddamn annoying. You're not the kind of man who takes life by the balls. You let your balls get stepped on. I should know, I've done it myself."

Lou gagged. Max rolled his eyes then glared at her. Paula smacked Lou square on the top of her head, and she hissed through clenched teeth.

"Not like that, you pervert. It was a metaphor." She sighed and turned back to Max. "Anyways, I hope you understand, sweetheart. No hard feelings."

"S-so you're going to let me go?" Max squinted, confused.

Paula laughed. "No."

He deflated. Lou wanted to giggle, but resisted the urge, given the gravity of their situation. She tried not to look at the bracelet lying in the corner, a few feet out of reach. With Paula in the room, there was no way they'd be able to scoot their chairs over. Max's gaze had steeled over, swallowing back every lump of heartbreak rising in his throat.

"Paula," he asked, "do you know what time it is?"

Paula frowned. "Do I look like I have a watch on me?"

"You have to take your heart medication at six o'clock." Max nodded in the direction of the small window. Tiny streaks of orange sunlight trickled through. "It's almost sunset. And in the summer, that's close to . . . eight, nine o'clock?"

Her eyes widened, and she grumbled under her breath. "Shit!"

"Yeah. *Oh shit.* You might want to double-check. Stressful day you've had and all, we wouldn't want you to keel over, would we?"

"Thank you for reminding me, Maxie."

She turned and walked out of the room, back upstairs. They waited for the door to shut before scrambling. The legs of their chairs screeched as they moved across the tile, inching closer to the bracelet. Lou leaned forward. Her teeth chipped against the edge of the counter as she bit down on the braided rope. Clenching her jaw tight, she turned back to face Max. She attempted to lean forward with the bracelet to cut through his restraints, but with her legs anchoring her in place, she couldn't bend forward far enough. She groaned in frustration.

"Put it in my hands."

He wriggled his wrists. His fingers were exposed enough that, if he had the bracelet, he could use it to cut through his own restraints. The only trouble was she had to drop it into his grasp. If she missed, it would end up on the floor, then they were fucked.

Lou scooched around. Her head craned forward, trying to perfect her aim before finally letting go. His fingers caught around the end of the bracelet and he held tightly to it. They laughed breathlessly, marveling at their accomplishment. Lou watched as Max weaved the bracelet across his bindings, and the individual sinews snapped away.

Then they heard Paula's stomping again, her pace brisker than before. They scrambled to scoot back to their original spots, and the noises from their chairs was almost deafening.

"What's going on down there?"

Lou pushed off against the floor again but her foot caught in a crack in the floor. She swore as her chair fell over and crashed against the ground. Max turned back to look at her, his eyes wide with concern, but she hissed at him—"*Turn around, turn around, hurry!*"—and he complied, keeping the bracelet out of sight.

Paula stampeded down the steps. A few strands of hair escaped her bonnet, sticking to her cheeks like flytraps. She looked at Lou on the floor and simply laughed.

"I'm not even going to ask how this happened. Today is not your day, is it, darling?"

Lou seethed in anger, but joy bubbled up in her chest when she saw Max going to town on those ropes. Paula didn't bother to right her chair. She stepped over Lou, joints audibly creaking, and approached the operating table. Rosalyn was still knocked out. Paula looped her mask over her face, powered up her electric clipper, and began to shave away her hair. Golden ribbons twirled in a gossamer dance as they fell to the floor. Dread flooded Lou's body.

It was too late for Rosalyn.

SIXTEEN

PAULA CONTINUED TO SCRAPE AWAY Rosalyn's hair until she was bald and speckled with bloody razor nicks. Lou watched as she retrieved what she could only assume was a repurposed heart monitor from one corner of the room. When Paula switched it on it showed an image of the human brain completely devoid of color. Word Art letters read out, "Procedure: 0%." A small EKG of her heartbeat was displayed in the bottom right corner. Holy shit. Was this thing supposed to measure the completion of the consciousness transfer? Had Paula built this rudimentary program herself?

Max couldn't cut through those restraints quickly enough.

Using a scalpel, Paula sliced a circular line around above Rosalyn's brow. She made a couple passes at this, trying to separate the skin from the rest of the skull. Blood trickled from the spot and Paula patted it away with little cotton squares that turned from white to burgundy. Lou couldn't help but be intrigued by her craftsmanship. Her grandmother occasionally performed surgery as a veterinarian, and although Lou had begged her as a child to go into the room and see what it was like, her grandmother never allowed it.

But watching all the blood and gristle from Rosalyn's skull drip onto the floor made her wish she had never asked for that. Paula wasn't being careful here; she was being callous. She muttered cuss words beneath her breath and tugged at the skin, trying to separate it. It split from the skull with a wet crack, reminding Lou of the sound towels made when you whipped them at someone. Blood cascaded down, splattering against the floor, and the heart monitor spiked, uttering a warning beep.

"Would you shut up?" Paula said to the machine. "I'm working here."

Out of the corner of her eye, Lou noticed Max continuing to work on his restraints, though his eyes were quickly filling with dread as he witnessed the horrors unfolding in front of him. Paula used a couple forceps to hold the skin flaps open before lifting what appeared to be a small power drill. Lou's knees trembled as she heard the cursed thing scream to life, shrill as a newborn babe. Clouds of white dust lifted from the hole, coating her gloved hands. As if that weren't enough, Paula lifted a scalpel, pushed it into the hole, and twisted it. Around and around she went, Rosalyn's skull the wine bottle and the scalpel the corkscrew. Blood continued to pour from the spot like a tree tapped for maple syrup. The monitor grew more concerned, its beeps louder and more consistent. Lou's stomach surged and she gagged. Burning acidic bile dribbled out from between her lips and her stomach seized as though she had been punched.

"Almost there," Paula trilled, clapping her bloodied hands together. Her voice was barely audible over the din of the monitor, but clearly, she thought things were going well.

That was when Rosalyn's eyes sprang open. She locked her gaze onto Lou, her mouth opening and closing in exaggerated movements like a hooked fish gasping for water. She murmured wordlessly, and her body twitched. Lou gaped, aghast. Paula didn't give her enough anesthetic, or it had worn off. Rosalyn's eyes rattled from side to side, unable to comprehend what was going on. The heart monitor spiked again.

"Paula!" Max couldn't contain himself any longer, the desperation thick in his voice. "She's awake. You have to stop."

Paula glanced down at Rosalyn's fishlike face. "Drat."

Rosalyn's swollen tongue thrashed against the roof of her mouth as though she was in anaphylactic shock. Spit bubbled from the corners of her lips and she moan-squealed, clearly distressed, voice fluctuating in pitch. Whatever Paula had done to her, it had destroyed her facet of language. The woman was still paralyzed, but her body convulsed in agonizing rolls of thunder.

"Stop!" Max shouted.

"I can't! Too far in." Paula continued to scoop and scrape with her scalpel, the tools clashing and clicking against the skull like dinner utensils. Rosalyn howled in a language transcending the human tongue. It was as if she were channeling the dogs who had cried out for her. Maybe she was. Stranger fucking things had happened today.

Spit churned in Rosalyn's mouth and turned into froth. White bubbles speckled her shivering lips. Eyes continued to dart back and forth in search of salvation. Holding back tears, Lou could only hope her mental apologies would reach her. *I'm sorry. I'm sorry. I'm sorry.* The heart monitor continued to wail, but Paula paid no attention to it. She grabbed one of the wires connected to the car battery and jammed it into the hole. Pink ooze squirted onto her scrubs. Rosalyn's convulsions grew more intense and her facial movements more erratic. Her entire body shook so hard the table beneath her vibrated. Piss soaked through the front of her dark jeans, turning them black.

"Oh, that is fucking *gross*," Max groaned, stifling a burp. "Oh, Paula, stop, I'm gonna be sick. I'm gonna be—"

"You shut up! I'm working here!" Paula screeched, her mouth opening so widely her mask fell off her face and drifted down over Rosalyn's eyes. Rosalyn thrashed her head from side to side, mouth open and bloody like a beating heart, and the heart monitor escalated in pitch until finally—

—a long tone followed.

Blood pulsed from the hole in Rosalyn's head, and the wire connected to her brain fell out, a granola-esque piece of matter attached to it. For several moments they remained frozen, the only sound in the room the buzzing noise from the fluorescent lamp overhead and the squelching sounds of blood and tissue escaping the head wound.

A single strained meow broke the silence, reminding them of its presence. A little paw poked between the bars of its cage, begging to be noticed.

Paula sighed heavily. "All this nonsense, and we still gotta use that goddamn cat."

SEVENTEEN

EYES WIDE, LOU GLANCED OVER at Max. His hands were still behind the chair. She couldn't tell if he had managed to cut through his wrist restraints yet. The bracelet wasn't on the floor, so it was still in his grip. With neither one of them free and Paula having an arsenal of drugs to choose from, their odds of escaping weren't looking good.

Rage boiled in Paula's eyes and she screeched, shoving the corpse off the table and onto the floor. More of Rosalyn's skull chipped off, and glutinous brain matter spilled like an overturned cereal bowl. Max pleaded with her to remain calm, his voice strained, and Paula responded by picking up a scalpel and whipping it at him. It narrowly whizzed by his ear and stuck firmly in the grout of the tiled wall.

Within the thick stench of copper permeating the room, Lou sniffed out something else: smoke. The orange streaming in through their little window was too intense to be normal sunlight. Sirens, distant but encroaching, echoed. Lou's heart sank to her stomach.

They had run out of time.

"Grandma," Lou pleaded. "You can smell that, can't you? You

hear it? The fire is spreading. We have to get out of here."

Malicious giggles escaped Paula's mouth. She rubbed her gloved fingers against her temple. Veins pulsated on her forehead and her teeth ground together, blood and white skull powder smeared across the canvas of her surgical clothes.

"I don't care if this whole entire fucking place razes to the ground. I want what was promised to me. I've worked *hard* for it. Your generation doesn't know a single goddamn thing about hard work. I've spent all my years in retirement studying, testing, slaving over the corpses of countless creatures and drunken vagabonds that stumbled my way. I'll be damned if things end like this."

"Well, prepare to have some bad news, baby."

Lou whipped around to look at Max again. He had pushed his chair back against the wall and reached a freed hand to grab the scalpel. He bent over and sliced through his ankle restraints with ease, dropping the bracelet to the floor. Paula's mouth formed a perfect *"O"* of surprise as he rose to his feet. With a huff, he rolled his shoulders back and cracked his neck, eyes filled with malice. The last time Max had looked at anyone like that was when Kenny Andrews had pushed Kelsea to the ground at recess in the fourth grade. Kenny's nose never looked right after that.

Paula smiled meekly. "Sweetie . . . I know you're angry, but you have to understand. I've been so frustrated."

She reached for another scalpel and attempted to walk closer to Lou, but Max staggered around the other side, arms wide like a bear on the attack. Paula yelped, scrambling to the opposite table. Max drew closer to Lou and stood behind her. He began to cut through the ropes around her wrists. In the background, the cat yowled, its little claws scrabbling against the side of the cage. Lou's heart shattered. Where had Paula found this little thing? Whose home had she kidnapped it from?

"We're leaving," Max said. "Now if you want, you can leave with us, but know that if you do, we're turning your ass over to the cops. If you stay down here, you can live out the rest of your life in freedom."

"*Excuse me?*"

Max smirked. "I mean, if you die now, you can get your do-over when you get to heaven. It's what you always wanted, right?"

"Bold of you to assume she's going to heaven," Lou grumbled. "There's an elevator to hell with this bitch's name written all over it."

"It's a figure of speech."

"That's not what a figure of speech is—"

"Do you want me to free you or not?" Max crouched down tc slice through her ankle restraints. Aghast, but also afraid, Paula coulc only watch as her granddaughter stumbled to her feet. "There we go We'll be on our way now, slutty buddy. Give my regards to your hus- band when you find him in hell."

Paula stammered nonsensically, startled by how all her plans were crumbling before her now. Lou couldn't help but grin. It was like witnessing the fall of a corrupted queen. *Is this how the French felt when they laid Marie Antoinette's head on the guillotine? Because this fucking rules* She squeezed Max's hand as the smell of smoke filled her nostrils She could see it drifting in through the cracks in the basement's foun- dation. They were surrounded, but they could make it out.

Max tugged her in the direction of the door, but Lou shook her head. "The cat. We can't leave it here to die; it doesn't deserve it."

"Oh, fine," Max huffed, letting her go so she could head over tc the cage. He kept his scalpel pointed at Paula, who glowered in re- sponse, edging closer. "Don't you fucking dare, hag. I've had just about enough of you."

"Maxie . . ." she crooned. "If you leave me down here, I won't blame you. But do you think little Loulou is going to stay in touch with you? Do you trust her not to leave you behind or throw you tc the cops herself?"

"If Lou . . ." Max swiveled his head around to look at his friend who was scooping the wide-eyed, shaking cat into her arms. "If Lou makes that choice . . . then you know what? I deserve it."

A pang hit Lou's chest. "*Max*."

"Well, I do." He turned to look back at Paula, who was now a few inches closer. "I saved her once, and everyone was fixin' to make me regret it. But nuh-uh. I did it once, and I'll damn well do it again."

"Too bad I won't let you." Paula's eyes stretched to the size of saucers and she let out a freakish battle cry, raising her scalpel high above her head. Max pushed her to the side but the blade nicked him in the shoulder. He groaned, one hand reaching up to stifle the blood squishing from the fresh wound. He twisted and jammed his scalpel into Paula's ribs. She howled. When she turned around to face him her feet skidded on the slippery blood coating the ground, and he stepped aside to let her crash onto the floor. She fell on her scalpel stabbed side, and the object rammed all the way inside her.

She could not scream, but moaned, writhing on the ground in pain. When her hands moved to lift her shirt, they could see the outline of the scalpel against her swollen belly like the handprint of a fetus desperate to escape the womb.

"Oh fuck," Max whispered, and his eyebrows rose. "That's gnarly."

For some reason, Paula pushed her hands firmly down on her stomach, causing the blood to gush out faster. The tip of the blade pushed through the membranes of skin, popping out on top, along with gristly sinews of what Lou could only assume were intestines, lined with yellow fat.

Lou squeezed the shaking cat closer to her chest and looked away. Blood bloomed from Paula's mouth, thin little rivers threading through her teeth. Max ushered Lou toward the door. The crackling of flames reverberated throughout the small space. The heat was sweltering, and their sweaty clothing clung to their bodies like plastic wrap. They had to move, and fast.

As they reached the door, Paula called out to them.

"Louella!" Paula croaked. "You're going to let your Grandma die down here?"

"You're not my grandma," Lou said, and her eyes watered with tears for the child she once was, one who wanted a normal grandmother who would take her on small outings and bake her cookies and knit her sweaters. A child who only wanted to be loved. "I'm disowning you."

As they attempted to exit again, a sound rang out: one heavy, meaty *thunk*. Confused, they turned to look back at Paula, but the woman's eyes had glossed over, dead. Her jaw was completely slack and her chest had stopped shuddering for air. Suddenly Lou began to feel woozy, and those God-awful black spots began to dance in front of her vision again.

Max gasped. "Lou . . ."

There was a scalpel embedded deep in Lou's back.

Paula had used all her strength to fuck her over one last time.

EIGHTEEN

LOU'S LEGS COLLAPSED BENEATH HER and with a yowl the cat escaped her arms, scrambling into the darkness of the basement. Max caught her before she hit the floor. A lump bubbled up in his throat as he gazed down into her pale face. She had been drugged, beaten, and now, stabbed. Her eyelids flickered, and her breathing was shallow.

He ripped his shirt off over his head, tugged the scalpel out, and watched her blood sprinkle on the floor like glitter. Grimacing, he pressed the cloth firmly against the wound, and felt the blood ooze from the space. *Fuck, fuck, fuck*. He tried to tie the shirt around her body, but he knew it wouldn't stay; it was too short and too thin. He crouched down, scooped her into his arms, and staggered over the threshold. He climbed up the steps. His hands became slick with her blood, but he did not lose his grip. Leaning against the wall for support, he kicked the door open.

Flames had started to eat through the walls of the house. The three cats on the bookshelf were now a pile of charcoaled fur. The German shepherd's eyes began to melt into its skull like bits of burnt chocolate. Dozens of frozen little eyes stared back at him in contempt and horror. He had to get Lou out of here, but how? Where had Paula put his keys? After scanning the room for a few moments, he spotted them hanging right by the door on their hook. *Thank fuck she remembered to do that for once.* "Lou! Grab the keys, Lou!" He waited with agonizing impatience for her to reach up and get them. He scrambled toward the door, coughing as the heat and smoke filled his lungs, and kicked that open as well.

Now outside, Max saw the wall of fire surrounding him. Sirens flashed in the distance—a good sign. The fire had eaten the back of the house first and hadn't reached the front yard yet. He scrambled over to his truck and laid Lou down in the bed of the vehicle before peeling the keys from her trembling hands. Her eyes didn't open, but her lips moved. The murmur of her voice was barely audible over the roar of the flames surrounding them. Max choked on his tears and leaned in, trying to listen.

"The cat."

He stared at her in disbelief. "Fuck me."

Max wiped the snot dribbling from his nose and sprinted back into the house. Flames devoured the living room, their greedy mouths gobbling the furniture and curated portraits on the walls. Overhead, the rafters simmered and crackled like an audience before the peak of applause. He scrambled back into the basement, eyes watering, and scanned the flickering darkness for signs of life. "Here, kitty kitty!" A soft cry pleaded for help from the darkness. "Kitty kitty! Hurry your ass up, we gotta go!"

Sirens wailed through the walls of the basement. Max peered into the darkness, making kissy noises, coaxing the cat to come to him. He spotted it beneath the stainless-steel table, curled up between the two dead bodies, its fur bristling.

"Come 'ere, you little . . ." he muttered, flattening himself against the floor. The cat hissed and swiped, but his hand clutched the back of its neck. It yowled as he pulled it out and into his arms. "I'm trying to save your life, you little fucker! Let's go!"

Green eyes glared at him with disdain, and Max rolled his eyes at the melodramatics before sprinting into action. Tiles popped off the walls and shattered against the floor. Flames licked the surface of the basement window, and the glass began to melt in long, wax-like streams. Coughing, he sprinted up the stairs as fast as his legs would carry him, and the fire nipped at his heels in response. He could feel his pants melt onto his skin. The individual fibers of his jeans blistered red and glued to his ivory flesh. He broke through the front door once more and sucked in air, hoping for a reprieve, but all that entered his lungs was heat. He spat onto the surface of his crumbling deck and sprinted into the yard. Lou lay in a pool of her own blood in the truck, her arms crossed over her chest. He opened his truck door, threw the cat onto the passenger seat, and peeled out of the driveway with a shrill shriek of his tires.

Only when the house was a twinkling star in the distance did Max allow himself to cry. Grievous sobs fled his lips. In the rearview, he could see a little glimpse of the truck bed. He whizzed by the firetrucks and hightailed it to town. The nearest hospital was fifteen minutes away.

He knew what would happen before they got there.

On the passenger seat, the cat looked up at him, slowly blinking. It sidestepped the center console, careful not to slip in the cupholders, and crawled onto his lap. Tears streaming down his cheeks, Max gripped the steering wheel with one hand, and used the other to stroke its smoky back.

ACKNOWLEDGEMENTS

Special thank you to Bri and Aurora for being my betas and braving this very strange, very disturbing story. Forever grateful for your friendship and your help.

Minnesota native Chloe Spencer is an award-winning writer, indie gamedev, and filmmaker. She is the author of *Monstersona*, *Duality*, and the upcoming paranormal mystery-romance *Haunting Melody* and adult horror novellas, *Vicarious* and *Mewing.* In her spare time she enjoys playing video games, trying her best at Pilates, and cuddling with her cats. She holds a BA in Journalism from the University of Oregon and an MFA in Film and Television from SCAD Atlanta.

Other Grindhouse Press Titles

#666__*Satanic Summer* by Andersen Prunty
#097__*Kill the Hunter* by Bryan Smith
#096__*The Gauntlet* by Bryan Smith
#095__*Bad Movie Night* by Patrick Lacey
#094__*Hysteria: Lolly & Lady Vanity* by Ali Seay
#093__*The Prettiest Girl in the Grave* by Kristopher Triana
#092__*Dead End House* by Bryan Smith
#091__*Graffiti Tombs* by Matt Serafini
#090__*The Hands of Onan* by Chris DiLeo
#089__*Burning Down the Night* by Bryan Smith
#088__*Kill Hill Carnage* by Tim Meyer
#087__*Meat Photo* by Andersen Prunty and C.V. Hunt
#086__*Dreaditation* by Andersen Prunty
#085__*The Unseen II* by Bryan Smith
#084__*Waif* by Samantha Kolesnik
#083__*Racing with the Devil* by Bryan Smith
#082__*Bodies Wrapped in Plastic and Other Items of Interest* by Andersen Prunty
#081__*The Next Time You See Me I'll Probably Be Dead* by C.V. Hunt
#080__*The Unseen* by Bryan Smith
#079__*The Late Night Horror Show* by Bryan Smith
#078__*Birth of a Monster* by A.S. Coomer
#077__*Invitation to Death* by Bryan Smith
#076__*Paradise Club* by Tim Meyer
#075__*Mage of the Hellmouth* by John Wayne Comunale
#074__*The Rotting Within* by Matt Kurtz
#073__*Go Down Hard* by Ali Seay
#072__*Girl of Prey* by Pete Risley
#071__*Gone to See the River Man* by Kristopher Triana
#070__*Horrorama* edited by C.V. Hunt
#069__*Depraved 4* by Bryan Smith
#068__*Worst Laid Plans: An Anthology of Vacation Horror* edited by Samantha Kolesnik
#067__*Deathtripping: Collected Horror Stories* by Andersen Prunty
#066__*Depraved* by Bryan Smith
#065__*Crazytimes* by Scott Cole
#064__*Blood Relations* by Kristopher Triana
#063__*The Perfectly Fine House* by Stephen Kozeniewski and

Wile E. Young
#062__*Savage Mountain* by John Quick
#061__*Cocksucker* by Lucas Milliron
#060__*Luciferin* by J. Peter W.
#059__*The Fucking Zombie Apocalypse* by Bryan Smith
#058__*True Crime* by Samantha Kolesnik
#057__*The Cycle* by John Wayne Comunale
#056__*A Voice So Soft* by Patrick Lacey
#055__*Merciless* by Bryan Smith
#054__*The Long Shadows of October* by Kristopher Triana
#053__*House of Blood* by Bryan Smith
#052__*The Freakshow* by Bryan Smith
#051__*Dirty Rotten Hippies and Other Stories* by Bryan Smith
#050__*Rites of Extinction* by Matt Serafini
#049__*Saint Sadist* by Lucas Mangum
#048__*Neon Dies at Dawn* by Andersen Prunty
#047__*Halloween Fiend* by C.V. Hunt
#046__*Limbs: A Love Story* by Tim Meyer
#045__*As Seen On T.V.* by John Wayne Comunale
#044__*Where Stars Won't Shine* by Patrick Lacey
#043__*Kinfolk* by Matt Kurtz
#042__*Kill For Satan!* by Bryan Smith
#041__*Dead Stripper Storage* by Bryan Smith
#040__*Triple Axe* by Scott Cole
#039__*Scummer* by John Wayne Comunale
#038__*Cockblock* by C.V. Hunt
#037__*Irrationalia* by Andersen Prunty
#036__*Full Brutal* by Kristopher Triana
#035__*Office Mutant* by Pete Risley
#034__*Death Pacts and Left-Hand Paths* by John Wayne Comunale
#033__*Home Is Where the Horror Is* by C.V. Hunt
#032__*This Town Needs A Monster* by Andersen Prunty
#031__*The Fetishists* by A.S. Coomer
#030__*Ritualistic Human Sacrifice* by C.V. Hunt
#029__*The Atrocity Vendor* by Nick Cato
#028__*Burn Down the House and Everyone In It* by Zachary T. Owen
#027__*Misery and Death and Everything Depressing* by C.V. Hunt
#026__*Naked Friends* by Justin Grimbol

#025__*Ghost Chant* by Gina Ranalli
#024__*Hearers of the Constant Hum* by William Pauley III
#023__*Hell's Waiting Room* by C.V. Hunt
#022__*Creep House: Horror Stories* by Andersen Prunty
#021__*Other People's Shit* by C.V. Hunt
#020__*The Party Lords* by Justin Grimbol
#019__*Sociopaths In Love* by Andersen Prunty
#018__*The Last Porno Theater* by Nick Cato
#017__*Zombieville* by C.V. Hunt
#016__*Samurai Vs. Robo-Dick* by Steve Lowe
#015__*The Warm Glow of Happy Homes* by Andersen Prunty
#014__*How To Kill Yourself* by C.V. Hunt
#013__*Bury the Children in the Yard: Horror Stories* by Andersen Prunty
#012__*Return to Devil Town (Vampires in Devil Town Book Three)* by Wayne Hixon
#011__*Pray You Die Alone: Horror Stories* by Andersen Prunty
#010__*King of the Perverts* by Steve Lowe
#009__*Sunruined: Horror Stories* by Andersen Prunty
#008__*Bright Black Moon (Vampires in Devil Town Book Two)* by Wayne Hixon
#007__*Hi I'm a Social Disease: Horror Stories* by Andersen Prunty
#006__*A Life On Fire* by Chris Bowsman
#005__*The Sorrow King* by Andersen Prunty
#004__*The Brothers Crunk* by William Pauley III
#003__*The Horribles* by Nathaniel Lambert
#002__*Vampires in Devil Town* by Wayne Hixon
#001__*House of Fallen Trees* by Gina Ranalli
#000__*Morning is Dead* by Andersen Prunty

www.ingramcontent.com/pod-product-compliance
Lightning Source LLC
Chambersburg PA
CBHW011508170626
46812CB00009B/3027
* 9 7 8 1 9 5 7 5 0 4 1 2 4 *